Benjie Johnson is thirteen, black, and well on his way to being hooked on heroin.

A lot of people would like to help . . .

Butler Craig, Benjie's "stepfather": "The kid got to hangin round those that's in a junk bag and then got in one himself. How he's to get out is what's to be dealt with."

Jimmy-Lee Powell, Benjie's friend: "Me and Benjie use to be tight. He was my boon . . . now he's soundin like from another planet . . . if I was in trouble like him, we would still be buddies. Friendship begin to split when one is caught in a habit and the other not . . . needles divide guys . . ."

Benjie's mother, Rose: "I wish I knew how to talk to Benjie . . . Be fine to tell him that something nice can happen for him in life . . ."

Walter, the pusher, isn't worried: "You may's well sell to kids cause if you don't they got some grown junky to git it for them and he's gonna take a cut outta they bag for hisself . . . No pain, I feel no pain . . . I don't feel sorry for a livin!"

And Benjie himself says: "If you 'on' somethin, that mean you hooked and can't give it up . . . I ain't hooked . . . I take somethin sometime, but I ain't no user . . ."

Other Avon Flare Books by
Alice Childress

RAINBOW JORDAN

A Hero Ain't Nothin' But A Sandwich

Alice Childress

AVON BOOKS
A division of
The Hearst Corporation
1350 Avenue of the Americas
New York, New York 10019

First Avon Flare Printing: April 1982
First Avon Books Printing: October 1974

AVON EOS TRADEMARK REG. U.S. PAT. OFF. AND IN OTHER COUNTRIES, MARCA REGISTRADA, HECHO EN U.S.A.

Printed in the U.S.A.

WCD   40 39 38 37

To Raymond and Cecilia

BENJIE JOHNSON

Now I am thirteen, but when I was a chile, it was hard to be a chile because my block is a tough block and my school is a tough school. I'm not trying to cop out on what I do or don't do cause man is man and chile is chile, but I ain't a chile no more. Don't nobody wanta be no chile cause, for some reason, it just hold you back in a lotta ways; unless you be a rich chile like in some movin picture or like on TV—where everybody is livin it up and their room is perfect-lookin and their swimmin pool and their block and their house and they also ridin round in one them quiet rollin Cads with a tape deck playin cool music and with air condition goin.

My block ain't no place to be a chile in peace. Somebody gonna cop your money and might knock you down cause you walkin with short bread and didn't even make it worth their while to stop and frisk you over. Ain't no letrit light bulb in my hallway for two three floors and we livin up next to the top floor. You best get over bein seven or eight, right soon, cause seven and eight is too big for relatives to be holdin your hand like when you was three, four, and five. No, Jack, you on your own and they got they thing to do, like workin, or goin to court, or seein after they gas and letrit bills, and they dispossess—or final notice, bout on-time payments—and like that, you dig?

Walkin through dark, stinky hallways can be hard on anybody, man or chile, but a chile can get snatch in the dark and get his behind parts messed up by some weirdo; I'm talkin bout them sexuals. Soon's you get up to leven, twelve and so—they might cool it cause they scared you know where to land a good up-punch, dig? I say alla this cause it's a fact. I don't go for folks cryin and bein sorry over me, cause I'm a man and if I can't take it, well, later!

Some cats moanin the blues, cryin bout how whitey does, and how the society does, and how they be poor and ain't got this and that. Answer me this: If somebody stomp you down and cuttin your air off so you can't even breathe your breath, you think they gonna let up just cause you cryin bout the stompin they puttin on you? Hell, no! Fuck the society! Thass what I say! Lass thing the society can do for me is to boo-hoo and come on with that sorry-for-you talk.

I hate for people to lie on me. No matter what they color or creed—I can't stand nobody lyin. Everybody can be wrong sometime, and when you wrong, you oughta stand up and *be* wrong right out, and not be hidin and lyin. When I'm wrong, I just be it. I ain't scared of a livin ass, not even if they kill me. Why folks got to lie and say I'm on skag, say I'm a junkie? My grandmother say, "You a dope fiend." I don't call her coffee fiend or church fiend. No, I don't do that. They lyin! If you "on" somethin, that mean you *hooked* and can't give it up. I ain't hooked. What's draggin them is that I ain't gettin off of it yet.

I don't mind too much when parents and schoolteachers, social workers and head shrinkers tag names on me and go to generalizin. They ole and it's parta they nature to be sayin things like they know facts and you don't know nothin! But, man, it can get to you when your best friend, least somebody you *thought* was your friend, talkin at you and sayin you on skag and how you better kick. When I hear the word "kick," I think bout somebody tremblin and shakin and vomitin and screamin and goin crazy. Thass not me. I *take* somethin sometime, but I ain't no user. Fact is, I used to skin-pop only on weekend cause I wanted to keep my mind on school and wasn't near ready to give up on the society. For a time I was even diggin bein a social worker, a block organizer or somethin like that. They got lotsa guys out there makin good money workin to turn the real addicts off and put em on the right track again. The ones who do that best are those who was once on theyself and then later shook it. They for real, cause they in on what the scene is all about. If I was a social worker, I'd know what is what and how to do cause I have dug the scene and didden have to be studyin it from a jive book.

It bugged me hard when Jimmy-Lee start layin them jive-ass heart-to-heart raps on me. Talkin like he already a social worker. "Man," he say, "straighten up cause you gonna kill yourself." Answer me this, if Jimmy-Lee is my friend and I'm his, then that make us equal, right? Then how come he talkin like he got it made and I'm lost? That ain't no way to be equal and reach somebody. He don't reach me a-tall!

One day I went all the whole day long with nothin cept a couple-a joints and a taste-a wine. I felt kinda strange, but I went the day and the night too. I went it, Jack! Comes mornin, and I'm pullin

myself together to go it some more. My mother
started in. "Why you so draggy?" she say. When I
don't answer and tryin to show my respeck by iggin
her, she keep it up. "I hope you not takin somethin
you should not have." She say it real nasty, and
slammin the fryin pan down on the stove, signifyin;
then she bang the dishes on the table so hard till
it's a wonder they didn't smash to bits.

All that kinda action is bad for my nerves. Fact
is, alla my family is nervous. My grandmother is
nervouser than anybody. She get up sometime and
walk back and forth, up and down the hallway, between her room and the kitchen, sayin, "Lord,
Lord, what is this! What is it all about?" She be
rubbin her hands together, shakin her head, and
stompin her feet. She little and skinny but stomp
when she walk, like you would expeck some fat
person to make so much noise.

Then my mother get nervous from hearin the
stompin and Grandma talkin to the Lord and she
say, "Mama, for God sake! For God sake! Keep still
till Butler gets his breakfast and get outta here."

Butler is kinda like my stepfather. I give him
credick for bein the coolest one mosta the time. He
talk just plain and easy, and he start off sayin to
me, "I'm not your father, but I have a thing or two
to say and gonna say it," then he would maybe give
some advice, or tell you what he don't like, but not
hollerin. The fact that he's "step" might be why he
ain't so nervous as us that's blood kin: he also don't
have much in the way of bad habits.

He like to have a bottle of Seagram Seven on
hand so he can take a taste-a that in the evenin,
while he sittin back listenin to a radio talk show
bout prejudice and race, and like that. Sippin his
Seven Crown, he says to me, "Listen and learn,

Benjie, time is changin, there's gonna be more op-
portunity." But he gets to my soul nerve when he
keep sayin that, cause I don't see him doin nothin
but bein a janitor in one of the whitey's downtown
buildins. Hear *him* tell it, he ain't no janitor, he a
maintenance man. Dig it, *maintenance* man ain't
nothin but a jive-ass name for janitor.

One night I say, "When they gonna have a oppor-
tunity for you?"

He shake his head and say how everything they
got goin is for youth. "It all youth program," he
say. "If you ain't young no more, the government
want you to drop dead and not be takin space and
breathin air."

Then I decide to sound on him, so I say,
"Nothin's goin for me but other people's mouth."
He say, "You oughta be hit in yours!"

Grandma then holler out, "Do it in fronta me
and you'll be in trouble!"

Then Mama say, "Butler is not really gonna hit
him! You and Benjie are both evil-minded."
Grandma went to slammin dishes, and Mama and
Butler start to quarrelin bout me. I get up and
went over to Tiger's place. Sometimes it's better to
fix yourself than to mess with other people.

Only reason I ever mainlined was on accounta
money, what you call economics. It take more skag
to skin-pop, cause the jolt is weaker then mainlinin.
Half as much mainlined will give a high like the
whole dose skin-popped.

I don't dig stealin or gettin into dirty action just
to get somethin for my nerves. It don't seem fair to
anybody and I been fair-minded all my life. I had to
take three bucks outta my grandmother's pocketbook, but I wasn't stealin it. Jimmy-Lee told me his
uncle was givin him ten smackers for a birthday

present. Jimmy-Lee bein my boon, I knew he'd lend me three singles so I could slip back what was borrowed before anybody found out.

One time his father had give him five bucks for school supplies, and Jimmy-Lee gave me a single for myself; it wasn't even a loan, he just say, "Here you go, my man, that's yours." We used to do that kinda smooth action, look out for one nother. Many a time I lend him my skates and don't ask for em back, dig? But the one time I cop somethin, as a borrow, from my grandmother, his ole, lyin uncle didden give him the ten. Fact is, his uncle went away on a cruise to the West Indies and act like he ain't never promise nothin! If he could go to the Virgin Island, why couldn't he hand Jimmy-Lee the ten? Answer me that.

I been catchin hell bout that money. Most times, when I'm wrong, I say it right out, but for some reason I stood there lyin, "I didden take it." I kept sayin it over and over, lyin like a dog. I ain't no chicken; but it seem like unfair to have three of 'em on me accusin like I'm their enemy, and they mine.

The real trouble is school and a jive-ass Black teacher name Nigeria. He pretend to be a Black Nationalist, but done turn Uncle Tom and got together with Mista Cohen, who is a Jew. The two of them did me in. Nigeria got the nerve to wear a black, red, and green button on his jacket. Somebody oughta rip the nationalist button off that spensive, British, hand-tailor suit. Nigeria Greene tole us he bought it in London when he went there on a vacation. He say, "This is what the English call a bespoke suit, and that means it's made to order." He's another one I once thought was for real. Wow, it cut through you, like a double-edge blade, when who you thought was a friend turn out to be stone enemy. Never trust a jive-ass nigga in a bespoke suit, specially one wearin a nationalist button.

The real dirty part is him gettin my mother and grandmother upset; after all, they only women. Look like the nigga woulda said, "No need to go to no lady bout this, I'll just talk to Benjie and see if we can rap out some kinda understandin." Sometime people don't know what they mouth can do, Jack! He hipped Cohen and the principal, then they notify my Gramma and she blabbin it all to my mother and Butler, then they jumpin in it. I'm the only one cool, cause if I wassen, I woulda tole the principal, the teachers, the social worker and the whole world that my stepfather ain't married to my mother no kinda way and that Nigeria believe in makin a all-Black government outta the United States: bet the law would say somethin to em bout that. But I ain't dirty, thassa fact.

BUTLER CRAIG

Stepfather

I've seen a lot in my lifetime, but never anything like this. Bein strung out on junk wasn't invented yesterday, no indeed, been goin on a long time, but damn if it ain't gettin worse. This the first time I've seen a child junkie thirteen years of age. I have heard of it, everybody has, and even heard worse; but I've never lived with it. I don't know what to do, and nobody else seems to either, no matter how much they be tryin, because there's too much jive talk bout "program" and "understandin." Damn, I *understand* it. The kid got to hangin round those that's in a junk bag and then got in one himself. How he's to get out is what's to be dealt with.

We can't put down nothin we hope to pick up again, cause now he's into stealin. Naturally, his own relatives are the easiest to rip off, cause we won't throw his behind in jail like strangers would.

These head-shrinker doctors pryin at his mother, wearin her soul out, cause their main hype is to find where to hang blame. A fact! They want every junkie to find somebody in his own house to blame. Always runnin down some jive bout "the society" on your TV, but when it comes to dope traffic and these not-yet-dry-behind-the-ears kids, all they

16

wanta hand you is jive questions bout do you understand the junky, or if he didn't get a red bicycle for Christmas, or if you took him to a baseball game lately, and a whole lotta shit like that. Yeah, it's shit, that's also what he's usin, and that's what authorities be shovelin at everybody. Social workers and head shrinks don't take kids home to their house after they get through plantin dumb ideas; they send them back home to rob their loved ones. Reason we can still find soap or a rolla toilet paper in the bathroom is cause he can't sell that for nothin.

Benjie is my stepson, more or less, and I have tried to take the *step* outta that and be as much father as he will allow. His real dad been gone for the last many years, ain't left no forwardin address, and ain't sent him no bread. Last Christmas he mailed a greetin card, with a damn, white-ass Santa Claus on it. He sign the card "Daddy" and put the date on it, but still ain't said where to find him; neither did he write a little note askin if the boy been eatin a meal lately or anything like that. All right, sometime you gotta forget and chalk it up to life experience. After all, maybe somebody didn't understand the boy's father. You can keep tracin down who didn't understand who, until you trace back to Adam and Eve. Damn, *nobody* ever understood me! I don't understand myself, and I been tryin to do that all my life. I damn, for sure, don't understand bein treated like a dog cause I got a dark complexion. Neither do I latch on to all this civil-rights-struggle jive. It ain't for real yet, dig?

Twenty years ago, down in Georgia, a white cat gave me a hard way to go, made me his target. That's how they do; might be almost decent to some other Black, but if there's a look in your eye, or somethin in your walk, that brings out the deep-down cracker thing inside him, then you in for a streaka hard luck. I heard bout white folks havin a "favorite" nigga, but there's more stories to be told bout who happens to be their unfavorite. This particular white cat used to low rate me with off-the-wall remarks; of course he was always in the company of some white buddy cats when he'd have a go at me.

I'd be comin in or out this crummy nightclub where I worked. I had me a saxophone, in those days, and doin a gig once in a while, when I wasn't helpin my uncle haul coal and wood. One day this shambly-lookin dude tripped me up when I was goin past him on the sidewalk. His friends cracked their sides laughin when he say, even before I could get up, "Nigga, why don't you watch your step?"

I dusted myself off and moved on. Some Black cats, across the street, went to talkin bad and tough bout what all they would do if it was them that got tripped.

"Man," they say, "thass dyin time!"

Some church folk standin near the corner, they say, "Best thing is take him to court, do it through N double A. Make a case!"

I didn't die *or* go to the N double A. Wasn't anybody left in our family but my uncle and me. He was a fairly young cat, single and solid in my corner. I took *his* advice, cause I dug it the most. We quietly bought us two plane tickets for New York City, and after a few days went by, we made our move. Caught that trippin-up cracker bastard one dark night and beat his ass almost inta the next world, then took our plane and got the hell out fore his mouth healed enough to report what happen.

Yeah, my uncle say, "Let *him* go to court and make a case."

I don't bother a livin, but I am very direct in my ways when they bother me. I am how I am, and I don't understand me any more than somebody else might, you see?

Me and Sweets work for every crumb we get to eat. If I could give her what all she deserve, she'd have it made. It make me mad for anybody to give her a bad time. One time she bought herself a leather handbag, with gold initials on the outside—R. C. That stand for Rose Craig. Rose is Sweets' first name, and Craig is my last. She got a nosey cousin who say, "What's the 'C' for? I didn't know you married again." Cousin was meddlin and bein nasty.

I said, "Craig is *my* name and I gave it to Sweets to use, if she wants it. When papers get legalized, and all like that, we can then go down to the courthouse and ask the law to sell us a license just so you won't have to be wonderin who's who and what's the 'C' for."

Cousin laughin that sick laugh people pull when they outta line and got put back in place. She say, "Go on, Butler, you too much!"

I laugh back how we do when we got somebody offa us. I say, "Yeah, I'm wise."

Sweets shake her head and talk kindly, "Yall cut it out, now."

People will go outta their way to sound on you when you mindin your business. The cousin is a fine person and studyin to be stenographer even, but she got too much mouth.

One time Sweets came down to my job to give me my keys, cause I had left them home. She looked fine in her suit and hat, also wearin gloves.

Neat! This greasy, white son-bitch who was fixin a steam pipe, say to me, "Who's your fine, roly-poly chick?"

"Watch your mouth, buster," I say, "that's *Mrs.* Craig, my wife."

Dude looked sick and started in to mumblin out a string of sorries. I mean, I do my best to keep down confusion bout the two of us. She looks right, she cooks right, and we suit each other in every other kinda way; so anybody don't dig the combination, tough luck! We satisfied.

Reason I work damn hard on a square job and hit the jam-crowded subway each and every mornin is cause I couldn't afford to support my habit of playin the saxophone, or the habit couldn't support me. One week you got a one-night gig, the next week nothin; then soon you find yourself jammin for free, just to keep your sound goin; and you be broke, broke, broke. Also I'm seein some best musicians, shootin up and drinkin rotgut, killin themselves like they not the greatest sounds in the world, a fact!

The rest of 'em out there hauntin whitey's footsteps, round recordin studios, beggin for a break in them casual, easygoin tones we put on when we gotta ask and ask and beg—for a break. They give you a break all right; will steal your music and pay themselves the profit. Other choices I had was to get out and find a hardworkin job, knock somebody in the head for their bread, or try to live off some chick and let her do the worryin and hustlin for me. So I work at somethin I don't like. I'm a home man. I dig a place where you can close the door and shut the people-eaters outta your life. Doesn't have to be fancy, a music box with a good sound, a name-brand bottle that can be tasted now and then, food in box, and a glad rag or two to wear when you wanta make a extra-nice appearance.

I try not to tangle with Sweets' mama. Sometimes, just as I'm ready for a minute of peace, to listen to a Coltrane record, while having a cold brew, that's the very minute the old lady starts singin hymns so loud till Coltrane ain't got a chance, no matter how high I'm turnin up the volume.

Sweets can't walk away, it's not her nature. That's her mother, and the boy is her son; she couldn't sleep nights if she left. But there's a distance growin between us. Poor folks ain't got many ways to solve problems. But if we had plenty money, her mother could go to a nursin home or have her own apartment, and the boy could be taken to a far place, like down South with some nice farmer people ... where there's no city nearby, just trees, air, fishin, and like that. Could live with middle-aged farm people who'll love him, feed him, and beat his butt if necessary.

It bugs me to see any more young-ass social workers. They ask too many questions. I'm not the one in trouble. It's a drag to work every day and then have strangers questionin you on your day off.

JIMMY-LEE POWELL

Benjie's Friend

Me and Benjie used to be tight. You see me, you
see him. He was my boon! No matter where I go, he
had to folla. Sometime I say, "Benjie, what you tag-
gin behind me for?" Be soundin evil, but he don't
care, he grinnin and sayin, "Goin where you goin,
that's where." He mean he don't have to ask no
questions, that wherever I'm at is fine with him.
Benjie used to make me feel good, like I was a
movie star or a basketball player on some big, winnin team, like the Knicks. Nobody could make no
bad cracks or be soundin on me round Benjie. It
was the same with me. I dug Benjie not bein jealous and jivin and holdin it gainst me cause I'm
smarter than he is in school subjects, and that I
made the basketball team and he didn't. Could read
in his face that he be wishin he was in on it with
me, but still glad I'm there!

Now he's soundin like from another planet, snif-
flin snot back up his nose, and eyes runnin water
while puttin the beg on for more bread. One minute
lookin pitiful, next minute mean and evil enough to
cut out your heart with a dull knife. Sometime a
junkie get mad with *you* cause he got a jones and

you ain't. That's why Benjie come down on me so hard.

"One thing," he say, "I ain't no chicken! If I wanta shoot up, I shoot! If I wanta stop, I stop! You a chickenshit!"

"Watch your mouth, boy," I say, "I don't play that game, and don't try to strong-arm me for my bread. We'll see who's chicken if you don't back up!"

Damn right he backed up. I can whip him, but I don't wanta. I'm feelin bad cause I give him his first jointa pot. Now I don't even smoke it myself, a fact, cause I got somethin else for a dollar to do; also, smokin, for me, is not such a fine gas. A high might be *the* thing for some, but it's just somethin I did to pass little time, and I don't have too much time to be passin because my brain is now into a lotta things. I don't dig turnin my head off and on like a water faucet. Also I don't wanta get caught off guard in this bad-ass wilderness, it's rough, and I want my wits woke, so I can find a better slot than the one I'm in.

There's some baaaaaaaaad studs out here, not strung out on nothin but nerve power. They hard-hustlin and doin everybody in, Jack. Who do you think they rob more than anybody else? The hophead, that's who! They will knock on a junkie for every dime he's got, they will also take his bread, promise to go get him a fix, and then never come back; the junkie then got nothin but a cramp in the gut and cold shakes. I tole Benjie, "No matter how much skag a guy gets, he will still feel low when he comes down, cause he knows that everybody is kickin on his ass and gettin themselves a case of the weirdo jollies outta seein him sweat for his next fix." Fact is, I seen a pusher make a junkie *beg* for his dose, before he would even sell it to him. You ready for that? Not me. All that talk bout bein a chicken, if you don't let somebody use your veins for a horse racin track, goes on past my head and I'm feelin no pain, dig?

I don't be preachin a sermon on the subject cause everybody don't dig bein told how dumb-ass they actin. To a cat that digs bein stoned, I say, "Right on, *kill* yourself, man." He be thinkin that sound good and will give you a full grin, like you his main boon. But I hate to hit down too hard on some these little junk men, cause many are good cats. Didn't junk knock Benjie down?

One time a guy name Carwell sold me some joints. I looked up Benjie, so we could try us a pot high. We went up the steps leadin to the roof in a house on the next block a beat-up, fallin-down place where we know ain't no super give a damn. We on the steps smokin, suckin in the smoke like we been seein and hearin bout. I'm little bit older than they are, makes me cooler than them. Carwell and Benjie takin off and goin on, "Uuuuuu-weee, um high, man. Groovin, this is it, man." I'm feelin kinda simple-ass cause all that ain't happenin for me. I feel sorta so-what—but no big thing. The roof door is open, and I could see blue sky and a white cloud straight up over my head, so it's there, dig? Remind me of the time I went in on a sixty-five-cent pinta wine—muscatel, it give me a headache hangover. Pot high, for me, is a dumb kinda don't-give-a-damn, but I know it's a high, and I'm sorta quietly lookin it over and tryin to figure it out. I got what you call a inquisitive mind. Benjie and Carwell, they makin talk.

"This it!"

"Live or die, make me no difference."

I'm layin back studyin sky and their voices ...
just waitin for the high to pass. Nothin left of me
but one dumb, sad feelin. I don't dig bein lost, I'm
better off found. Carwell say, "I know a stud who
buys grass by the bag!" I don't like Carwell, his
eyes ugly, hard brown buttons. You got to *stay*
stoned to stand Carwell a-tall, I'm still not likin him
even with the high on. Losin yourself is for some,
but it ain't for others. It ain't for me.

Benjie had a long stringa spit hangin offa his bottom lip. I'm lookin at spit, seein sky through a roof
door, and turnin my bread over to the button-eyed
Carwell. It ain't for me, dig? I really don't need no
knockin out. I'm sorry how Benjie is now gettin
caught up and expandin on the program.

A social worker is somebody who makes they
bread and fame offa other people's troubles. Lotta
people plannin to make it as a social worker, cause
the field is so wide-ass open, and trouble, accordin
to Benjie's grandma, is somethin that's sure gonna
last *always*. Hell, I could be a social worker myself!
When a junkie gets real messed up, the thorities
send them into talk groups to get talked to. What
you think they talkin bout? Just tellin how they
papa and mama don't understand, and they also be
sayin "ghetto" and things like that. Benjie gonna be
brainwash with that crap. Right now, he try to tell
me how his daddy run off and how that make him a
child from a broken home. Shit! Sometime I wish
my home was broke. Benjie don't know how to dig
good luck! He's got a stepfather who's bringin in a
color TV and hi-fi record player and all kinda good
things people need. True, Mr. Butler Craig gives
him talkins to bout don't do this and don't do that,
damn, the man titled to say somethin. But Benjie

steady complainin bout havin a step and a broken home.

I got a real father, but Mama say Daddy surely been broke on the wheela life. She talkin bout the Freedom Rides that used to happen in the South. My father was into all kindsa action, picketin and breakin down segregation at food stands and in bus stations and like that. He went on a March to Washington way back in 1951. He say that was the *first* time Martin Luther King spoke in fronta the Lincoln Memorial. Daddy got a certificate that look like a ten-dollar bill; it say, "This is to show that James Lee Powell went on the March to Washington for Civil Rights." Papa say he went down with A. Philip Randolph leadin New York marchers. Mama say, "Your father has been a part of whatever he thought might make us free, and his head has been whipped more than once. One time they turned our car over and set it on fire. He's broke down from peaceful protest."

Daddy belong to the old school, thought they could make white folks feel shame bout how they did us. He been a left-winger, that means a Communist, a Socialist, a Liberal, a Nationalist, or a Democrat. He's now what you call a Independent, that means you can change your mind from time to time. He's forever ready to jump into a new bag if it's what he calls "a promisin-lookin thing." He ain't got much time for me and Mama. He reads his books and go to talk on the corner as a stepladder speaker, speech always question society and the law. He can solid preach! Old guys dig him. My father is forty-three years old and the old fellas still call him "Youngblood." He ain't gonna buy no color TV cause he don't hang onto one job long enough to buy nothin. Mama, by herself, is steady bringin in

money for the bills, He always gonna kick somebody's ass ... and has been known to do it. He wake
up evil sometime and cuss and slam doors. Mama
say he been through a lot, but I don't go for too
much door slammin.

He got books bout Garvey, Malcolm, Karl Marx,
Du Bois and Martin Luther King, history books
and Africa maps. He say, "It make me mad to work
for a dumb-ass white man who don't know nothin
a-tall." He quit a laundry truck job, the post office,
and many others. When he got money, he's free-
handed but he hardly ever have any. He kicked a
hole in the bathroom door one night—and ain't nobody done anything to him. Mama was stirrin some
hominy grits, she never even look up, just keep
stirrin.

A white teacher name Mr. Cohen is the one who
taught me to read good and fast, but he didn't
know, cause he doesn't notice what's goin on half
the time. I never learned much bout readin in the
lower grades, cause all we did in my P.S. was bring
in and sneak-read what we please, like dirty
comic-strip books where funny-book characters all
screwin each other, and like that. Some teachers let
girls bring in love story magazines and even let us
all play cards. You could do anything if you kept
your voice down and did it quiet. That was how
third and fourth grade went by. Teachers would
use the period to get their absent-present files
straight. When Mr. Cohen got holda our class, he
was mad cause our readin was not cool a-tall. Every
day he made us get up, stand to one side of the
room, in a line, and do nothin but take turns readin
out loud. It was like ridin a bicycle; one day, after
bumblin and stumblin, I started to read fast and
easy. I just knew how and been goin on ever since.

The Cyrenian Promise Baptist Church

SENIOR CITIZENS!
Read your BULLETIN BOARD before asking
questions!

SPECIAL ANNOUNCEMENT
Our pastor, Reverend Holsom, regretfully
announces the cancellation of all mid-
week evening meetings, due to purse
snatchings and holdups perpetrated
against elderly members as they leave
the premises. As many activities as
possible will be rechanneled to fit into
the daylight hours of Saturday and
Sunday afternoons. This Monday Reverend
Holsom and a committee of concerned
citizens will visit our local precinct
captain to demand —

1. More and better police protection in this area.
2. An end to drug traffic in this
   area.

Join us at 9 A.M. in front of the
church. Last week one of our elderly
members was robbed and beaten as she
left a night meeting of the Scholarship
Fund Society. This is only one of many
such shameful incidents which have
occurred in this community. Send Get
Well Greetings to Mrs. Ransom (Elizabeth) Bell and offer up prayers for her
continued fine recovery.

MRS. RANSOM BELL

Grandmother

This house is my jail, only I pay rent. I'm afraid to go out in the street alone, day or night. Bad boys now hate old people and will beat them and take away our little money. Bein old is strange to me, cause I'm not yet used to it. I have sat in the narrowness of this room, my hands folded in my lap, lookin at the knuckles and veins of my fingers; they seem larger, knotty-lookin, my mind tell me that's old. But if old was only looks, then old could be better dealt with. Old is also *ailin*, you get a sudden jab or pain in your shoulder or knee joint, and that pain be so perfectly sharp, it's like somebody stabbed a long, hot ice pick right down to the bone. That'll happen three, four times in a row; then when I brace before it stabs me again, it'll lie low and not come back for a while, or it'll hit in a new place, like the back of my knee or the hip joint. That's how ailin goes, you can't depend on how or where it'll happen next. But old is also more than pain, I guess. Maybe old is your mind goin one way whilst you go another.

All my life I been hearin bout old folks and, of course, old folks is always somebody else and you can understand that much better than when you might be the one. There's a part of bein old that's got nothin to do with aches and pains, you get sudden thoughts that flash in from no place. Thoughts can hurt like real pain. Thoughts will not hang together long enough for me to sort them out and think a matter through, cause just as I'm handlin one thing it flies away and another will pick up where the first left off, only it's different—and that's how I get mixed up.

I'm so glad I got Jesus! My personal Saviour, the Son of God! Jesus Christ is a waymaker! When your enemies press in on every hand, and they sit in the seat of the scornful, and when there is no heat in the radiator of this top-floor walkup, and when my onliest daughter is hummin and sighin past me like a express train passin a freight, when the man she's livin with, in sin, and callin her husband, is drinkin whiskey in the presence of the Crucifixion picture on the livin-room wall, when my grandson is stealin from me to buy dope, when they leadin me, gainst my will, to go make paper flowers at the old folks' club, when others pickin my clothes out for me and I'm not likin what they buy, when won't nobody take me to church, when all the nice people I know are dead and gone, when bad boys rob me in the street and knock me down, when all these things come to pass—as predicted in the Scripture; bless the Lord! Even in the midst of my heartache, light shines in on my soul, and I am truly lifted! The walls of this little room just roll back, and bright glory shines everywhere, in my heart, in the air; round the mirror glass on the wall turns glinty and sparkly, and a glassa water is a glassa diamonds!

Yes, they hit me and knocked me down, my own kind did it to me, but I'm still alive. Don'tcha see

how good God has been? Who would I have if I
didden have Jesus! Never did I know I'd live to see
a time like this. I wake up in the night and hear the
next-door jukebox playin that loud, bad-rollin music, kinda tunes make folks think about sexin, drinkin, and stayin up all night and bout usin bad language on each other. They play the drum like they
swingin the hammer of Satan, thumpin it up gainst
a cement wall, nothin but thumpin and no music in
it. I be layin here, tremblin in the dark, but just as
confusion is bout to smother me off the face-a the
earth, I suddenly feel and know that Jesus, the
natural Christ, is here in this room. He is here re-
mindin me that I have claimed Him as my *personal*
redeemer. Jesus is *here,* promisin life everlastin!
Then confusion takes flight on the wings of angels. I
chase that evil jukebox sound outta my head by
singin from one hymn to another—"How Great
Thou Art" and "Precious Lord Take My Hand."
Suppose I had not been saved by the Blood of the
Lamb? I mighta been in the insane asylum because
bad boys mugged me in the street. It is the object of
sin to drive you right-straight-clean outta your
natural mind!

When I was a girl, down in Mississippi, my folks
was sharin crop, we was poor, but there was some
little good to it, cause I had the lovin service of my
father and sweet mother. My father was a strong,
good man and not like these triflin ones who are
signs of the end to come. My mother was a wom-
anly woman and knew how to sew clothin and can
peaches, if and when she had some to can. My father got kill in a argument with a man who
wouldn't pay him money that was owed for his
hard work. Some said, "Too bad he had to lose his
life over collectin a little bitta money."

My Mama say, "Many die from the cancer, others die from the double pneumonia, and some go when they drop dead from the heart failure; but my husband died from a case-a righteousness, and he look a heap better in his casket than them that naturally shriveled away between the sheets." She was proud of my father.

The Lord puts things on us to see how much we can bear, sometimes we fail the test and don't bear too well. My Mama say, "Everybody ain't Job." Look like our family just went downhill after Papa was buried. Mama sent one child to this relative and the other to that, then went off workin in domestic service so she could send us money. Wasn't long fore she followed Papa to the grave. The way we chirrun was scatter around, the double death just cause us to scatter more, everybody had to hit out for theyself.

I saw one brother once when I was dancin in St. Louis, Missoura. He was railroadin through as a Pullman porter. Lord knows I'm sorry for my beginnins in young womanhood, but if you don't know, you don't know. There was two ways I could choose, do housework for white folk or be wife for some man. Only man that brought up the subject of marryin, at that time, was one who lived out in the country, a sorta mud hole of a crop-sharin place, and he had a few hogs and chickens of his own. He was upstandin, everybody say, but I didn't wanta cover any ground that I had covered before. Sharecroppin killed my parents, so that was bout enough of it for me.

In my day there was a dance called the shimmy, some called it the shake, and all who did that dancin, for pay, was call shake dancers. That was what I did. I learned how to stand up, with my hands

over my head, stiffen out and shiver every parta my
body all at once, and also one part at a time; even
could make my bosom tremble while the rest of me
was still. So I got a job doin that in a after-hour
place where people come to dance, sing, drink boot-
leg whiskey and listen to the jazz. After-hour places
was illegal, but the colored couldn't work in fine
legal places. I wore silk dresses and fancy underwear with fine lace, and I'd lift my skirt to show
the lacy underwear and then go into the shake,
shimmyin one part at a time, then all parts. It's a
wonder I didn't hurt myself, cause I had to do it
four or five times a night, then wait table servin
whiskey and fried chicken dinners. I received lots
of rude proposals and drunks used to try and feel
me, but I had made up my mind to live better than
was expected, so I didn't encourage them. The Lord
was graciously guidin my footsteps, because I got to
meet my husband, who was a bricklayer who happen to be layin brick for the after-hour front fence.
I sure didden have any hard luck about him. Ransom was his name, we got on fine, was married and
came on North.

Up here, he couldn't get no bricklayin to do cause
it was a all-white union. But we managed, he promised never to let anybody starve us off the face-a
the earth. We rented a big eight-room apartment on
Seventh Avenue and took in roomers, workinmen
who also took meals with us. Ransom learned how
to write policy slips and collect bets people make on
number playin.

We only had the one child, our Rosie. She was
still little when Ransom died from TB. You never
grow too old to miss love . . . I sure miss Ransom.

BERNARD COHEN

Teacher

I'm whitey, I'll be the goat, okay? You have no idea how things go down when you're whitey in a Black setup. I go out to work every morning, like a lamb to the slaughter.

I got to contend with the students, the school board, the parents, the teacher's union, the Board of Ed., the PTA, the principal, winos on the block, the pushers, the hall monitors, and in particular, this one Black teacher who is the local Gestapo, with Black Power, like crazy, all over the emm-eff community. His name is Nigeria. No joke. He didn't become a take-a-new-name Muslim or anything like that. His parents named him *Nigeria*, even before Black, Black, Black hit the country.

Nigeria Greene is a pain in the ass. He's built like an oversized football player and walks down the hall like he owns the U. S. of A. and all that's in it. He teaches the bottom of the seventh grade, and I have the top. Got the picture? He gives his students a workup just before they hit my class. They come to me, at the beginning of the term, with eyes narrowed down to slits, they loll back in their seats as if to say, "Okay, motha, unroll your program and see what it gets you." He turns out a mean-ass,

34

cold-hearted crew. All over his classroom walls are
pictures of Black people—Marcus Garvey, Du Bois,
Robeson, Harriet Tubman, and also many slaves
who knocked off whitey in order to get free, and so
forth. Was *I* ever a slave master? Did *I* bring slaves
over here? Did *I* ever lynch a Black? Am *I* the
one?

Of course they have special needs. I put up pictures too, Frederick Douglass, Booker T. Washington, Ralph Bunche, even a picture of Malcolm X,
all different kinds, something for everybody. They
walk in, look the pictures over, then slap hands together, laughing like they're in on the joke of the
year. You can't know what it's like to feel their
contempt. Nigeria Greene passes my classroom,
pauses in the doorway, and says, "Right on!" The
students call out in a casual way, "Hey Africa,
whatcha know!" They never directly like to call
anyone or anything exactly what it is because, in
their minds, that would be "square." Because his
name is really Nigeria, they call him Africa; that
way they're not calling him by his first name, and
they can avoid saying *Mister* Greene. They used to
rudely call me "Mista Charley," I took offense at
that and told them to stop. One boy said, "Take it
to court and fight for your civil rights like everybody else gotta do."

From nine in the morning to three in the after-
noon, feels like I'm wading my way through a pool
of cold molasses. I've started to quit, but then I get
to wondering if Nigeria and his kind are trying to
make me run. What will this country be if the all-
Black schools get all-Black teachers? If we give up
our seniority by default, they will move on to the
assistant and principal jobs like—like Grant went
through Richmond. Is it healthy for kids to learn

nothing but Black history, Black supremacy, and Black power?

True, it's wrong to treat them unfairly, and I definitely uphold their right to be taught *some* of their history. In the past, I have wholeheartedly signed petitions to have more Blacks integrated into jobs where they have previously been shut out, the building trades, electrical unions, and so forth. But, in all fairness, I must say that in education we have absorbed more than our share of Blacks, we really have. A few more Nigeria Greenes, and we will succeed in cutting our own throats. What about *my* right to work? Are we to eliminate ourselves? I hear many whites complain about supporting *them* on welfare, but I know for a fact that there are Blacks who would like to take all the best jobs and support *us* on welfare.

Let the know-it-alls talk about busing or not busing, but I wish they would start busing teachers and leave students alone. I could stand a change of scene once in a while, without having to quit my job.

Added to the general hostility are the pushers around here selling pills for a dime each, ups mostly. Kids can drop pills in a soda or a glass of milk right in the lunch room. Pot, horse, and cocaine are also a part of the scene, but acid seems to be a whitey habit. In all fairness, I must say, kid addicts don't bother a soul, they don't. A junkie nods on off and lets you alone, when he's fixed. But don't leave your money or wristwatch where he might get to it when the dose is wearing off.

Nigeria Greene called me to one side and raised hell about Benjie being on the nod.

"Hey, man," he says, "you gonna let him ride the

horse? A boy is hangin off his desk and you ain't made move the first."

Nigeria likes to say "ain't" even though he knows better. That's *their* way of trying to invent a language because they don't have one. He's also trying to impress the kids, make them believe he's a swinger and one of the crowd. At the moment he's in a big hassle to get a Swahili class started. What in the hell do they need with Swahili? Well, maybe they can use it to ask for a welfare check in two languages. I don't really mean that. I'm just tired of catching hell from Monday to Friday. There are a few other white teachers on this floor, but they are buddy-buddy with Nigeria and seem not to know what to think until he gives them the word. There's another white guy down on the second floor, but he's a racist. Last year the parents drew up a petition to get him out, but somehow or other he couldn't be dropped. The other whites are women, a few bleeding hearts, some check collectors who don't give a damn how the school system is run, and a couple of zombies who have grown old in the obedient service of the Board of Ed. Zombies wear the ugliest shoes ever made. They drag through the hall to the teachers' dayroom, carrying tea bags and cardboard boxes—to brew tea and snack sesame crackers. Try to enlighten them about current conditions, they shake their heads and start talking about a sabbatical.

I've tried to relate to Nigeria, but we can't communicate without having an argument. When he gets angry, his eyes go bloodshot and that bushy Afro seems bushier. "What do you want from me?" I said. "Remember I'm whitey. Nobody needs to hear me call Benjie or any other Black kid a junkie." I had to sock it to him the same way it gets socked to me.

He said, "Benjie is one of the best kids we'll ever see. If I could save him, I would—"

There's nothing to do when people shut me out. Some of the more refined Black teachers are cooperative and kindly, but they're clannish, too, when it comes to race matters, afraid of taking the part of a white person when another Black is in the picture.

My wife is forever planning to move out of the city. She never suggests any definite place, but nightly keeps the subject going along with dinner and through the CBS late news. When I suggest a place, she thinks it too far away, too dull, or too anything she can imagine. What she'd really like is a ten-room colonial house on a tree-shaded acre of ground in the center of the city, with two armed guards patrolling on twenty-four-hour service. The constant topic is crime in the street, muggings, and Negroes, Negroes, Negroes. On the other hand, she looks at pictures of the ones in the New York *Times,* those who are advisers to the government or the UN, sighs and says, "You must admit a lot of them *have* something, three strikes against them, but they still have something."

I had hopes of ignoring the race business, functioning at full speed and forging the way for better education. But now the Puerto Ricans want Puerto Rican teachers, the Blacks want Black, I'm afraid to run and afraid to stay. Everyone is for sale on a new auction block, which is the ground underfoot, wherever we stand.

If mayors, governors, and Presidents can't put a stop to drugs, why should anyone ask me, especially Nigeria Greene? Benjie was a fine boy, one of the best, in disposition. When the others acted up in class, Benjie looked at them, looked at me, then ended up looking out of the window. He must have been determined to remove himself. At any rate, he has.

BENJIE JOHNSON

BENJIE JOHNSON

When I was a chile, me and my mother was cool with each other, got along just fine, also got along with my grandmother, who was a classic dancer when she was young. My mother used to help go over my homework and we be watchin our TV too: Do little homework, then look up and dig TV when the chase go on, or the mystery bout to be solve and the bad guy caught. I had me a happy childhood. Mama and me used to go for a walk on Satday night, go to the newstand bout ten o'clock and buy the Sunday newspaper with funnies in it, then we go to the candy store and buy us two little boxes of hand-dip ice cream, one for her and one for me, each gonna have our own box to eat outta while we read our papers. Sometime Mama say, "Let's go all the way!" Then she laugh and we go to the bakery shop and buy coffee ring to have early Sunday mornin.

I never did dig coffee to drink, but it smell fine when it perkin on Sunday. We be eatin our coffee cake with the raisins inside and nuts on top, and I have cold milk with mine. Sometime we don't have coffee cake, and Grandma make a bacon pancake. First she fry your piece-a bacon till it's criss, then she pour pancake batter topa that, so your pancake gonna come out with a piece-a criss bacon stuck in the middle of it.

Back in them days, we used to know when we was happy and didden have to be talkin it out to *see* if we was. Mama used to have a happy look right on her face. Grandma used to sing a hymn call "Will There Be Any Stars in My Crown?"—sing it on Sunday mornin while makin our bacon pancakes. Mama say, "When you gonna dance for us? Benjie, your grandma ain't never danced for me in her life."

Then I tease Grandma, "I don't believe you can dance!"

My grandmother take hold the end of her skirt and say, "A-one, and a-two and a-three!" Then laugh and say, "Fooled you, didden I!" She really didden fool nobody cause we knew she wasn't gonna dance. Grandma say, "My dancin days over."

Christmas time we had a nice tree and plenty fruit and candy. I'd get games and new clothes. Only time Mama look sad is when she say, "It's terrible for a woman to be alone."

I look at her and ask, "How you alone if you got me? You got me, Mama!"

She smile and say, "Sure have. You mine and I'm yours."

All that was back when I was six, seven and eight, back before Butler took over and stole my mother. Back in days before Nigeria Greene pulled the big double cross. I'm sorry I ever had him for a teacher. He really ratted.

NIGERIA GREENE

Teacher

This guy across the hall from me is not to be believed. He is white, and in this school because the system makes damn sure to have white representation in every nook and corner of the country, the world, and, in particular, in every Black community. Look around your city and let me know if you see coloreds represented fifty-fifty in the white community. No, it doesn't go down that way. I'm sick of explainin and talkin race. Race is the story of my life and my father's life, and I guess, his father and all the other fathers before that. As a kid, I was in on "race" discussions in school, at home, in church, everywhere. It's a wonder every Black person in the U. S. of A. hasn't gone stark, ravin mad from racism . . . and the hurtin it's put on us.

My grandfather was a Garveyite, a dues-payin member of the UNIA—United Negro Improvement Association. He talked my mother into givin me the name Nigeria. People used to call me Gerry to get around the pure African sound, but my name comes on fine these days.

As I said, Bernard Cohen is not to be believed. His whole mission in teaching is to convince Black kids that most whites are great except for a "few"

42

rotten apples in every barrel. It burns me to see white teachers bend kid's ears with the same tune, year in and year out. They'd rather ruin their lives by makin them think they're imaginin the game bein run on them than to save them with truth. You can face hardship if you realize it's not all your fault and you are dealin with some things that have been deliberately dropped on you.

Most of the kids don't talk anything but Harlemese, but have minds as sharp as a double-edge razor. They laugh at textbooks because most invite laughter. "Our" school is fulla white-face books written by white writers. Only two pictures on my wall when I came here ... George Washington and Abraham Lincoln. Abe was, at least, involved with the Civil War and the Emancipation thing; but George was a slaveholder, and it is impossible to hang George over my front blackboard and not discuss him. When I discuss him, I don't go by what's in these history books or we'd be dealin in lies. George was a slaveholder, and he had it put in his will to free alla his slaves *after* his death. But he owed a slave woman whose cookin was so fine that he freed her while he was livin. She musta really known how to barbecue!

Well, that time slot is over and outta our hands. But now is now, and I don't need a slaveholder lookin down on thirty-seven Black students, while I'm teachin history and civics lessons.

From a kid on up I was good at history. I mean I was good at memorizin what was put before me and was a whiz at recitin it back. If the book said a lie was truth, that lie was the answer I put down on my test paper. I learned that from my father. He was slick as a greasy whistle and yessed his way into the post office. It was hard for a brother to get

in durin Papa's early years. You had to know somebody. Fortunately, he knew books were full of lies
and never minded tellin me so, but he would also
say, "Tell the lie back, tell 'em what they wanta
hear, cause it's their book and their school and they
will fail you if you don't write it down the way it
reads. They'll do you outta the chance to earn
yourself a crust of bread." Then he'd tag on the
clincher, "Futhermore, if you don't bring me a
good report, you gonna get outta here and labor
hard because I won't support no full-grown man."
He meant it too.

He was sincere in a hemmed-in kinda way and
dealt with life exactly the way it was laid out,
playin the game according to old, tested rules. He
was a trustee of the church and took up collection
every Sunday mornin. I can see him now, standin
at attention, holdin the mahogany plate, his brown
face lit by sunlight shinin through a stained-glass
window. One Sunday I noticed the window was a
picture of a sword-carryin, golden-haired angel,
with snowy, feathery wings. The other windows
also showed whites as saints and angels, none
looked like my father or any of our people; there
and then I began to find Black Nationalism within
me, to realize there was no integration in God's
heaven, and that I must accept even the Christian
rejection of me and mine. I felt hatred for that evil
God who made us sing, beg, weep and pray for
humble admittance into his white heaven.

I decided to correctly give back all the silly answers required of me. I promised myself to make a
day when I'd teach what could not be found in my
schoolbook, teach how to search for and find with-
held truth. I had to have a piece of paper labeled
diploma in order to enter this so-called house of

learnin where Black children are shut off, shut out
and shut up, forced to study the history of their
white conquerors, this peculiar place of white facts,
white questions, white answers, and white final ex-
ams. I couldn't explain it to my father, because
Grandpa's Garveyism had skipped right over his
head and landed on me. I left Dad to enjoy what he
had, the Saturday night poker game, Sunday morn-
ins with stained-glass angels, lodge meetins, all the
rituals which kill time from one holiday to the next.
We saw the New Year in by eatin peas and rice for
good luck. If peas and rice were lucky, we'd be
free! My folks had the Fourth of July at the beach,
Thanksgivin Day with my aunt in the country. Mis-
ery was almost sweet, plenty of finger-poppin and
dancin—in between folks bein killed, chased, shot
at, segregated. I finger-popped along with the rest
and ate my share of souse and sweet potato pie. But
I had me a plan, Nigeria Greene was gonna be the
Black Messiah of the classroom, gonna light the
way with Blackness. I try to do it. I try, like Nat
Turner said, "because it pleases me to try."

But, as I was sayin, Cohen, across the hall from
me, is not to be believed. Give him his due, he
teaches hard, when kids leave his room, they take
somethin with them, even if it's a lie. He has a
tough hide to take what some-a these roughs can
put on you, but spends mosta his time tryin to undo
what I taught the term before. Mainly, he wants to
make it clear that he's "not the one" who's doin us
in. I've heard him sing that chorus so many times.

"Yes, there were slave masters, but *I'm* not a
slave master. Yes, there is exploitation, but *I'm* not
an exploiter. There are good and bad in all races,
Skin color has nothing to do with social wrongs, all
groups have been enslaved. . . ."

I have to get my class strong enough to weather his storm. I've confronted him about this time after time. "Hey," I'd say, "why you messin up minds? What you layin on my people? Sound like you teachin us to sing a new song ... 'God bless segregation and all that it's done for me.'"

He gave me a lotta sass. "Why do you slang talk?" he says. "Are you trying to prove that you're one of the elite underprivileged?"

"Right on," I said. "I'm one of the underprivileged, and I dig Black talk, I smile Black, think Black, walk Black, and all the Black that's not yet discovered is out there waitin for me to find it. You get off my kids!"

We go on like that sorta half jokin but meanin to draw blood with every dig. The oldest white folks' strategy is to attack a person in a way that looks fair. Dig how the Indians got washed away and labeled "hostile." It shakes Cohen to his boots when he hears me ask, "What time is it?" And the class hollers out, "It's nation time!" I'm teachin that it's high time to straighten up and hold hands because my inner clock is tellin me that now is only half past slavery.

I'm only hopin they can *hear* me. The enemy has turned off so many eardrums till some of us now hear only through the bloodstream. No stuff, brains and ears are turned off for the duration! If somethin *feels* good or puts him to sleep, that's all the turned-off brother needs to keep him quiet as the grave until grave time comes.

When I use this segregation they have laid on us, use it to bring us closer and wiser in Blackness, Cohen screams about "segregation in reverse!" I held a two-period rap session on that accusation. "How come it is," I say, "that when whitey pushes us off to one side through law and mass muscle, that is segregation, but when we get to usin our enforced togetherness, they call it 'segregation in reverse'?" Then I go to cookin on the subject and clarify for them. "What they mean," I say, "is that when segregation works against us, that's what it's suppose to do, so it's in forward, but when it starts to work against *them*, it's in reverse, meanin that it's goin the wrong way. You see, whitey is not ever gonna say *he* is bein segregated against, that would be too much like what happens to *me*. That's how come it is he yells that it's goin into 'reverse.'" When the hurtin is on us, it's in forward; on him it's in reverse.

Three teachers, two *Negroes* and one white, made complaints to the principal, the gripe was that I am "creating an atmosphere" which breeds hostility. I told them there would be hostility in this school if I had never been born. Dig?

Cohen wasn't in on the complaint because he tries not to stick his head in an electric fan when it's turned on. He also remembers how we almost went to swingin fists when he complained about my givin spellin lessons instead of stickin to history and civics. I challenged all the "expert" opinion that "inner city" children can't read. I told my class, "Yall can read and write, so don't hand me no jive. When I go in the toilet and note the handwritin on the wall, I have yet to see 'fuck you' and 'shit' spelled wrong, nor have I had any hardship in understandin those lines scrawled bout who did what to who, so if you can read and write dirty words, you damn sure can read and write all the rest."

Cohen's complaint resulted in the principal givin me a talk about "decency and morality in teachin methods due to the vulnerability of the young . . ."

and so forth and so on. I wasn't ready for that, not
ready for any white principal from a surburban-
split-level-livin-segregated-Anglo-Saxon   neighborhood to question my morality values, specially
when he's makin his daily bread in a dirt-poor, so-
called Black Community and spends his pay in
West Park Gardens Drive, or wherever the hell
else he buses out to when the bell rings at three
o'clock. I cooked on him, "It's middle-class subur-
banites who have been makin all the immorality
news here of late," I say, "the ones playin switch
partners with one another's wives. We, in the
ghetto, think it's not nice to do that kinda thing.
You folks got slum minds."

I give Cohen lots of air and plenty good room except to keep him in line when he needs it. My wife
tells me to cool it and don't try to change the world
all at once. Maybe I need some criticism, but so in
hell does she. Why does she go to fashion shows?
The community is fulla these clubwomen givin
fashion shows at downtown white hotels. Who cares
what kinda lace somebody is wearin with their silver fox jacket? Too many hardworkin chicks spendin bread and time on white satin with ermine linin
and all the crap. When I read the Black press, I
almost choke. Constantly givin champagne sips
and one-hundred-dollar-a-plate dinners and costume
balls and comin-out parties. Comin out from where?
Our folks holdin meets and dances down at the
Bunny Club. Why would a woman wanta look like
a fur tail is growin outta her butt?

Oh, so much gets to me! I keep seein this kid,
Benjie, noddin over his desk when I pass Cohen's
room, justa-sleepin and hangin. I walk in, look him
over, and walk out. Cohen is gettin hot under the
collar; so am I. Finally, I take Cohen to one side

and tell him the boy looks stoned. He gives me the
TV line. "Kids sit up all night watching late TV,
when they get to school they have to rest—"

I cut him off. "Don't run that game on me," I say.
"Let's take him downstairs and turn him in."

Cohen pulls stubborn on me. "This is a class," he
says. "I'm not turning in anybody. The parents get
upset, the principal gets upset, the kid feels be-
trayed."

"Right," I say, "but let all that happen rather
than see the boy dead, let's don't kill him outta the
kindness of our hearts."

We look Benjie over and spot a couple of needle
marks. I say, "You been into anything you
shouldn't, little brother?"

Kid says, "I'm cool, Nigeria." But his cool is too
stoned. Cohen and I take him down to Principal
and request notification of parents. Benjie backs up
ugly and says, "You a traitor, man! Yall pickin on
me cause I'm Black." He really cut up, called me a
Oreo Cookie, that's Black on the outside and white
on the inside. I wanta knock him down, cause that's
my nature, but instead I take his bad mouthin.

Newspaper item:

Fabulous Fashion Show and Dance

The La Paloma Femme de la Jours held their ninth annual ball, fashion show, and champagne sip downtown at the gorgeous Metropolitan-Cadrington Arms Hotel on Saturday last. The Royalty Room, of which there is no whicher, was decorated with amazingly lifelike silver and white doves, their feathered wings stretched in full flight. Each bird bore a white orchid in its golden beak. Ten silvery, gleaming, electric fountains spouted out the bubbly, to make a most magnificent merry for a very worthy cause.

The best-known names from political, social, literary and entertainment worlds were present as snowflakes in a blizzard. Three bands, rock, jazz, and calypso, played a variety of now and then sounds. Our illustrious mayor made a gracious, albeit belated, entrance to commend the La Paloma Femme de la Jours for their compassionate, humanitarian work. Finally, the president of the elite club presented a $250 check to Mrs. Nigeria Greene, the lovely treasurer of the Friends of Drug Fighters Alliance.

ROSE JOHNSON (CRAIG)

Benjie's Mother

I try to keep the neighbors out of my business because every friend has a friend, and if I can't keep a secret, how can I ask them not to tell what I told? When you're full of silent troubles, people sometimes think you're crazy or standoffish. They talkin to me bout two-for-one food sales at the supermarket, and I'm answerin, "Oh, that's too bad, you have my deepest sympathy." That's because another person just told me about a death in the family. My mind stays confused these days. Well, maybe troubles should not be kept secret, might be better if we shout from the housetop, but everybody is too ashamed and so we ha-ha at trouble ... to keep from lettin on.

There's a woman downstairs from me whose husband beats on her like he's fightin for the heavyweight crown, but she tells people she tripped on the sidewalk. Cross the hall is a neighbor who's coughin up his lungs, but he keeps talkin bout his "asthma" and buying cough syrup and nose spray. Top-floor apartment got a young daughter who's expectin, with no husband in sight, and they talkin bout him bein in the service. Then there's Emma Dudley, chasin after every man she sees while tellin us how many she has to turn down. All tryin not to see what's here to be seen. But each and every one is blessed beyond understandin, cause they don't have a child who's on drugs—like I got.

The school brought me the news, but I had been suspicious before, but the thing seemed to get by me because you hate for a child to believe you always thinkin somethin's wrong. Maybe I haven't been takin enough time with Benjie since meetin Butler, my common-law husband, but Butler's been takin time. He bought tickets for a ball game so they could go together like father and son; I'da gone too, but here lately my mother been turnin on the gas and forgettin to light it with the matches, another time she left bath water runnin and flooded the downstairs apartment. Butler is not one of those men who can't stand the stepchild because it's not his. He'd be crazy about Benjie if only the boy would let himself be liked, but the child is contrary and actin like he can't stand anybody.

Benjie was on the way at the time Big Benny and I got married. My in-laws had a fit because, as they put it, "He's young and has the whole world before him." Wonder what they thought was in front of me ... besides a baby? I've seen it time and time again ... folks feelin like their sons are gettin bad deals when their girlfriends get pregnant. I bet that's why families don't wish for girl babies much, cause they can grow up and get pregnant. People like boy children cause they can carry on the family name and also cause they are not the ones who ever have to have babies. I have even seen folks put she-cats out cause they're gonna have kittens. When kittens and puppies do get born, everybody wants a male one, if they want to take any a-tall.

Mama made me haul Big Benny into court. I had

to almost cry blood before they awarded me fifteen dollars a week. Ben would pay one week and skip two; finally, I stopped goin to court about it, and the payments went down from once in a while to never. Mama had to put most of her money in the house for rent and food. Truth be told, it was her apartment in the first place. I went out to the factory ... sewin on a power machine, turnin out flags and pennants for baseball games and political rallies.

A few years back, I took on a extra job helpin out a caterer on weekends, servin private dinner parties, weddings, anniversaries, and like that; that's how I met Butler. He was servin drinks so he could save up for a car. Poor fella never managed to get his car. He was a Godsend to me in more ways than one. He's who I shoulda met in the first place, but I never did do anything right the first time around. Butler was the one lucky break in my life. Mama likes him too except for one or two matters. Fact is, he's the only one I've met that she could stand a-tall. She was so mad bout the way Ben treated me till she feared for me to trust anybody again.

I love Butler, from when I met him four years ago, right on up to this very day. No matter how our troubles go, I shall love him right on for all that he has been and done for me. He is my dependable love through thick and thin. He is strong and dark like cigar tobacco, and always ready to put himself out to help another person, to try and see things from their point of view. He looks good. When he laughs, his eyes crinkle shut and he slaps his hands together because he's enjoyin that laugh like it's the best thing in the world. When we go to the beach, I like to sit under the beach umbrella so I can watch him take that first dip in the water by himself. His body is firm and tough from hard work. He gets up, stretches his arms in the air, then says, "Wellllllll, guess I'll get me some-a this water, try it out, see if it's too cold for you chickens." He goes runnin down to the water's edge and plunges in without toe testin, goes right in over his head, and comes up with a whoop, a holler, and a laugh, "Wow! Cooooold!" That's how he does bout everything. Butler says, "If you into somethin, *be* in it." Nobody has to sit up nights wonderin and guessin what he means.

Me without a divorce, last year we just did the best we could, made a life together without legal papers. He is standin by my side before these teachers, social workers, and doctors, without anything legal to back him up. If you don't think that's doin a lot, try dealin with officials. They are legal crazy! The worst sin in the world is fine with them if it's legal.

I wish I knew how to talk to Benjie. I feel shy or ashamed when I want to speak my real feelins. Be fine to tell him that something nice can happen for *him* in life, something like how it is with me and Butler. One day I almost said it ... after goin over the words in my mind, "Benjie, the greatest thing in the world is to love someone and they love you too." But when I opened my mouth, I said, "Benjie, brush the crumbs off your jacket."

A child thinks his mother should be a mother and nothin else. Trouble is they been taught, all of us been taught, that love is for squares. Guess me and Butler don't look very special in his eyes ... just a plump lady and a hardworkin man goin along doin their best.

THE PRINCIPAL

Walking through these corridors, I remind myself that in three years I'll be ready for retirement. I have done some good in my time and would like to leave with my sanity and pension. I look forward to peaceful moments in which to write this definitive book on better methods of education.

In this school we have Blacks, whites and Spanish-speaking students and teachers. Our assembly programs have been planned to cover them all and the topics of the day, civil rights, economics, Vietnam, the vote, the draft, racism, nationalism, Communism, Socialism, welfare, homosexualism, women's rights, transvestism, a free Puerto Rico, Pan Africanism, the UN, Black capitalism, Zionism, Cuba, China, the Soviet Union, the religions of mankind, and so forth and so on. There aren't enough weeks in the year to cover the subjects. There must also be time slots for holiday celebrations, Christmas, Chanukah, Lincoln's and Washington's birthdays, Easter and Passover, Mother's Day and Yom Kippur, Columbus Day, Thanksgiving Day, and Brotherhood Week. In this school we also observe the birthdays of Martin Luther King, Jr., and Malcolm X, Puerto Rican Heritage Week, and Afro-American Culture Week. This morning I received a delegation requesting assembly programs for the observation of Oriental and Eastern cultures.

We manage to have a track team, a school band, a student newspaper, a Parent-Teacher Association, a Committee of Concerned Parents, a karate class, and an adult-education evening program.

I have outlived two teachers' strikes, three student rebellions, and one community riot. In the past few years theft has become a deepening problem. We have suffered the loss of office equipment, sports equipment, and even our American flag was stolen from the assembly platform. Anything that can be sold is likely to be stolen. I keep wondering: Who would want to buy a "hot" flag?

Handling teachers requires much tact. Mr. Cohen regularly threatens to leave. He is not the most diplomatic person I've ever met, and yet, mysteriously, the highest percentage of good readers come out of Cohen's class.

Mr. Nigeria Greene is definitely a Black Nationalist problem. It's all I can do to restrain him from painting his classroom walls black, red, and green—according to him, "Black for our color, green for the land to which we must return, and red for the blood which must be spilled to attain it." He has fashioned a philosophy from equal parts of democratic socialism and Garveyism, both generously sprinkled with the sayings of Mao Tse-tung.

He has fewer dropouts and less absenteeism than any other class, the highest library attendance, and his boys are the backbone of our track team. Bernard Cohen and Nigeria Greene do not get along very well, but the kids fare a bit better because they're both here.

Drugs may be illegally purchased anywhere, but there is an immediate, negative reaction on the part of the public when any specific school is mentioned by press or television. In one school a boy died from an overdose of drugs, picket lines surrounded the block, and the public clamored for a change of principal and staff members. Then came protests from citizen committees and the churches. When it all blew over, everything became as it was before, nothing changed, nothing accomplished. Parents are afraid of the dealers who poison their children; parents are afraid of their children. I share the same fears.

Experience has taught me to avoid the subject, except for the occasions when we have a scheduled visiting speaker who gives us an assembly talk on drug abuse. Very often the speaker is an ex-addict. I get an uncomfortable feeling that he is being projected as a heroic figure, and I fear that some of our students may see drugs as something to use and then bravely give up. The speaker does not mention that he is one in a hundred who was able to kick the habit ... after all, it is the nature of each human being to think of himself as a one-in-a-hundred person.

We think of poverty as a condition simply meaning a lack of funds, no money, but when one sees fifth, sixth, and seventh generation poor, it is clear that poverty is as complicated as high finance. One gradually learns begrudgingly to respect the poverty-stricken: They have endurance; they push their vitamin-starved bodies on and on from one day to another; they continue to stand up under humiliation and abuse. Some buy ridiculous, high-priced, impractical clothing ... on the installment plan, hoping to hide poverty behind fake prosperity. The racketeers swagger; they strut; putting on a show of indifference, looking down on the rest.

They exploit each other, bleeding the weakest to obtain gaudy consumer goods for themselves, "the Cadillac poor," trapped, caught fast here, forced to live side by side with their victims. Seeing these things, all I can do is push education while the pusher pushes heroin.

Cohen and Nigeria brought the boy to my office. Those two men who have never seen eye to eye on anything got together to bring one more straw to this poor camel's back. The boy's face told the story; he had turned us off, and now we had the job of turning him in. I did it smoothly. His grandmother came first, giving us a long lecture on the ways of God; his mother and stepfather took him to Harlem Hospital with my signed referral for detoxification.

Each day I remember to praise honor and dignity, celebrate worthy heroes ... and bear in mind that I shall soon reach the haven of retirement. No matter what I do or don't do there are drug addicts.

Newspaper item:

Drugs Available in Local Schools!

It has come to the attention of this reporter that drugs are readily available in at least one local grade school. One child, age thirteen, was spirited out of the building while heavily under the influence of narcotics. The principal is obviously trying to avoid scandal and responsibility by hushing up the incident. When we tried to reach him by telephone, he was "not available" according to a woman who nervously identified herself as a "clerk" in the office.

Certainly all concerned parents should protest this state of affairs to city, state, and federal officials. Our children must not be further victimized by ruthless pushers and timid school officials. Those incapable of guarding youngsters within the school should resign or be removed regardless of tenure. Community organizations, what say you? It is time to strike out against death! It is time to . . .

WALTER

The Pusher

The pusher, the pusher, that's all you hear! They don't call no other salesman a pusher, but that's what he natural is ... a pusher, no matter what he's sellin. Your TV set is fulla pushers tellin you to run right out and buy cake, candy, cars, soft drinks, beer, pies, and whatever the hell else they can talk you into buyin. Dig it, *they're* the pushers, not me. I don't push cause I don't haveta! These early-risin junk men be lookin for *me*, dig? I ain't said for them to "run right out" and buy nothin! But they runnin, and if they can't find me, they gonna find somebody else fast. Push? You outta your head? I don't let em know where the hell I live else they'd be clawin and knockin at my door, or in the street scratchin theyself and callin up at my winda; Hey; Walter!"

Alla these cryin-Emma social workers rap out lyin jive bout the "poor addict." Dig it, ain't nobody ever held down nobody else and shot him in the vein. The damn law is fix to give a "user" less time for pushin than a "nonuser." Dig it, nonuser means *clean,* and that's what I am. I don't shoot no shit in my arm! I handle it, look at it, cut it, sell it, and risk having my ass thrown underneath some

60

lonesome jail, but I don't shoot up in myself and don't sniff nothin either, cause I damn sure know it'll eat the linin outta my nose. Dig on, I have tole junkies show skag blows health and mind! Like the cigarette pushers print on the package how it can do you harm, that's how I tell what junk can do. Talk bout tracks on your arm—hell, man, tracks ain't nothin. Your vein will close up tight and then you gotta find another vein to hit. You oughta dig some ulcerated sores, them that's got runnin holes in they arms and legs!

If I quit pushin tomorrow; you think any junkie is gonna do without this poison cause I didn't show? You need a straitjacket if you do! From city to city, town to town, from block to block and house to house, there is someone who will get you anything you want, if you got money! Talk bout pushin, I'm pushin for cops, when you get right down to it. You heard me! When I pay off, what the hell you think I'm payin with? Payin him outta my sales. I got to hustle ten bags before I can pay the fuzz five singles, dig? So I'm pushin for the law. If he hands on a little taste to the next fuzz-on-high, who's collectin offa him, that means I'm out here pushin for both of em, dig it? Been days when I paid off in front, before sellin even one bag—that's how rough the game is played. No, I didn't say *all* cops; all I can tell bout is who I pay. But dig this, when you pay fuzz, you ain't spendin much time wonderin who's like this and who's like that; the cat you pay is where your mind's at. What I know is I got cops pimpin off me.

You may's well sell to kids cause if you don't, they get some grown junkie to get it for them, and he's gonna take a cut outta they bag for hisself. No pain, I feel no pain bout this soft-hearted song they

singin bout the "kid" who's an addict. If I had me a
kid, his Black ass would be home in bed at night, in
the day he'd be in school, and I'd trouble myself to
see to it, dig? I wouldn't be shufflin no soft-shoe
dance and callin for the thorities! Trouble is, these
tom-ass parents want me to be lookin our for their
children while they mama is out on the street
playin the single action. Their papa, if they got one,
is drummin up sixty-seven cent for a pinta wine! If
you don't believe me, stand round and dig the
scene. They want me to be the baby-sitter!

I don't feel sorry for a livin! If I was to get
bumped or go to jail for life, these crackers who
own the world and all what's in it would go right
on doin like they been doin, just as if my ass had
never been born. They haulin horse into the States
by the ton ... ain't most of it gettin here in nobody's suitcase, or sewed up in a dollbaby ... that's
some dumb-ass idea yall done picked up from TV.

Sometime I feel sorry for a guy who's carryin a
monkey, but I don't feel sorry long. Feelin sorry
ain't good business. Junkies be wearin out my
feelins and gettin into me for a free fix. Oh, yeah,
yall don't hear bout the times you trust the lyin-ass,
knowin damn well that soon's he gets a buck, he's
gonna deal with somebody else and duck you till he
run outta shoe leather. It's like this, weak is weak,
when some dude is weak and keep feedin his weak-
ness, he's done for! Yeah, he is, I say it's all over
but the service and the flowers. Most times ain't
gonna be no wreath cause they gonna plant him in
a pine box that don't cost no more than the price-a
two fixes, the state give him that free on-the-house,
then they dump him with the rest of the unknown
dead, inna big hole, and plow em all down together.
If the niggas stuck together that close when they

was alive, they could move the world. Potter's field,
that's where they get together.

Yeah, some do *kick*, but ain't but so many can do
it. Although they all can walk round leanin over,
scratchin, noddin, and talkin bout what they *gonna*
do, I give em encouragement. "Do it man!" I say.
"Do your thing!" I be sayin that while I'm slidin
their next fix outta my sham cigarette pack. But
when I be callin them weak, I still don't mean
dumb, even though they into a dumb action. Some
junkies supersmart. They talkin baaaaaaaaad, they
rap out the history of the world, and tell what it's
gonna take to get whitey's foot offa your neck, and
what is a revolution, and what mistakes was made
by Garvey, King, and Malcolm ... but they can't
keep their veins closed, dig? So they be rappin and
noddin and boostin and buyin and comin out here
every mornin funkier and more raggedy than the
day before. Yeah, they walk that fallin-forward
walk, that slack-kneed shuffle, tippy-toein along,
eyes searchin round to see if somebody put down
somethin they can pick up and sell.

When a mainliner is high, he feelin biggety with
nothin to feel biggety bout. His underarm might
have a sore in there, or he got a abscess on his gum
or his groin, or he got maybe a case-a the double
syphilis, could be his bowel ain't moved in two-
three weeks cause horse constipates ... but he's
grinnin and rappin bout his groove. What the hell
you want from me? He killin himself in his own
way. It's a free country, right? If the nigga ain't
gonna be or do nothin, he may's well nod away. Let
him hold up his mama to keep with his habit ... so
long he don't hold *me* up. If one lay his hand on
me, I'll kill him quicker than skag. I hate the nigga
most much as I'm hatin myself; the both of us ain't

had no more sense than to be born Black in the middle of some big white action.

I ain't the only one hustlin! Woman down the street is writin small-time policy ... that big, fat-ass Black sista sit there eatin a dozen pig feet and five poundsa greasy potata salad—man, that's just her lunch! Come dinner she send her kid to the corner to buy four ordersa ribs with the hot sauce and french fries. She got her number customers lookin up their dreams in a "dream" book ... pawnin their weddin rings to play the daily single action ... trying to hit that digit. Children got nothin to eat in the house ... they livin offa Kool-Aid and crackers, plus what they can lift ... while moms is waitin for the big "hit." Kids meanwhile comin down with ringworm and pellagra. Everybody lookin for a quick miracle ... some easy kinda way to make it without buggin whitey too much.

Don'tcha know that if a fix could fix things, I'd shoot skag myself? Nothin is for free ... not even a *feelin*. Somea these whiteys usin horse cause they feelin bad bout how good it's suppose to be for them but they seein how it ain't goin down that way. The parents done sent big brother's ass off to get murdered ... smiled and waved "good-bye" to the boys. "Send him to the Army, that'll keep him outta trouble." They pushin war, dig it? Ain't no way to live without pushin somethin. They ain't stopped horse from ridin through the Army—or anywheres else.

Me, I say screw the weak and screw the power. If it's call free enterprise, then let it be free. Nother thing, If I had my way about it, I wouldn't be related to a Black-ass nigga on this earth. All them that wanta die let em put a five in my pocket, and I'll help em to slowly make it on outta here, with a smile on their face ... and one on mine. Less of them makes more room for me! The hell with the junkie, the wino, the capitalist, the welfare checks, the world ... yeah, and fuck you, too!

BENJIE JOHNSON

It like bein in jail. They askin questions and keep askin the same ones, then go on to somethin else, then final double back and ask the first question when they think you mixed up and forgot what you said. The mainest thing they wanta know is how and where I got skag. You can get it just bout anyplace, but I ain't gonna squeal ... and even if I did, the connection might not be there when they go to check him out. Sometime he ain't there when *I* get there. Connections float and change their scene, if they don't they'll get washed away in a sudden clean-up action.

What I did, I did, I don't blame anybody. Anyway, only one I know who's a connection is a fella name Walter. I met him through a guy call Tiger. Me and a boy name Carwell, we cut school and went up to Tiger's pad to buy us a joint to smoke. It ain't really Tiger's pad all to hisself. Is his aunt's house. She be out workin a sleep-in job and come home only once-twice a week. Tiger's mother is in a hopsital gettin over some kinda breakdown, so this place is just bout like almost his own. Tiger is fifteen and a baaaaaad cat. Tiger is makin hisself money. If you know somebody, like I know Carwell, they can get you into Tiger's place cause they known to Tiger. It's comfortable and pleasant if you

need a place to be when you cut school. When you
cut, you got to go someplace, and it's hard to sit in
some abandon apartment buildin that's ratty-smell-
in and cold. If you try to get into a pitcher show,
they will turn you away if it's a weekday and before three o'clock, that's cause they can lose their license. If you go in the park and try to sit out in the
cold, the plainclothesmen might pick you up. They
got plainclothes and uniform fuzz who do nothin
but go round the park and see who they can catch
that might be up to somethin. They will pick you
up and ask how come you not in school. The Black
ones do it just like the white. Carwell say a pig is a
pig no matter what color. So you kinda lost if you
cuttin and got no place to wait it out till after three.
We went up to Tiger's. He don't charge you
nothin for comin in, and it's a nice, clean, warm
place, with a good record player and a TV. Tiger got
wall-to-wall on the floor and drapes at the window
... also venetian blinds ... the bathroom got pink
shower curtains with green sailboats all over it. Is
one fine-lookin place. Tiger don't allow no gamblin,
or dancin, or girl action and like that. Tiger say he
don't wanta wise the neighbors and turn them
gainst him by havin noise goin on. Fellas just be
sittin round having a smoke, they buy the joints offa
Tiger. You can also buy little cake and candy and
bottle-a Pepsi. Tiger say he keep the operation
small so he can quick clear the place when his aunt
comin home for her time-off days. On them time-off
days she be hangin more fine curtains, cleanin, and
waxin everything neatly and makin pillows and slip
covers. Carwell say she hopin to someday be home
and joy her fine-lookin house for Christmas and
other holidays. Tiger got special afternoons when
he sell dogs with pickle and mustard. But whenever

it's his aunt's time-off day, he puts a red sticker on the wall in the downstairs vestibule. If you go to his apartment when the sticker is up, he open the door and say in a loud voice. "Man, you got the wrong place, ain't no Tiger live here!" His for-real name is Gerald, but nobody call him that except his aunt and teachers at the school. When he talks loud and winks his eye, you know not to stand round and give trouble.

So this time when we went up to Tiger's, there was boys sittin round on the floor with works, they cookin horse and shootin up. Tiger say all that's happenin is a little skin-poppin. "Say, my man," Tiger say to Carwell, "why don't yall pop a taste and stop wastin your bread on gage. Smoke don't do nothin but make me burn up my strawberry incense trying to put down the smell."

Everybody laugh and Carwell say, "No man, I ain't ready for that, me and smoke is doin all right."

Slick-lookin, light-skin boy name Kenny who live over near my block, he say, "Fact is, Carwell, we gonna call you Chicken Little."

Nother fella say, "Don't be so hard on him, man, maybe he tryin to set a good zample for his little titty-fro friend."

Since it was me they callin titty-fro, I thought I'd try they bluff. I was really hopin they wouldn't gimme none, but I say, "Kenny, I'd take a light hit, but I ain't got but seventy-five cents."

Tiger look me over and say, "Right on!" Then he tell the fella that's doin the shootin, "Give the little man a hit, don't make it but a touch, cause we don't want no amachures to overdose on us." I was out there then and had to go it on through or else look like a big mouth who had to back down. Kenny gave me a toucha the needle, and first it seem like nothin was goin on, then next I was hot and cold and my heart went to boppin fast and my head drew tight. They were all watchin and Tiger say, "Damn, man, you got nerve."

"I say, "Shit, ain't nothin."

Kenny say, "It might make you puke, kid."

I laugh and wave my hand like I know the score. I say, "Well, sometime life be that way." They fallin out laughin and diggin me like crazy.

I like how they watchin me and payin their respeck, lookin at me like they know somebody fine when they see him—not just sittin back like I'm nobody. I kept waitin to be sick, but I wasn't. My head got to feelin funny, and after while I went to the bathroom, just in case, but all I felt was queasy and strange. Guess shootin is for feelin nothin. I didn't care what and just sat there, my heart thumpin inside and me wonderin. Every time I thought bout home, my mama come to mind. She is really okay. Gotta admit I dig that Butler sometime too. But they don't need me round. On Satday when they be joyin their day off, they goin out to the movies and say to me, "Hey, you wanta go to the show, too?" They always say "too," and when they say it, I'm thinkin that me as the one more would be one too many. I always say, "No, I got me a TV think I wanta see." But, dig it, who wanta be the extra one goin along to eyeball some picture bout Black people bein poor? I dig movies where people got high-rise hotels and where they be international spies wearin they fine suits and hoppin big planes from one airport to nother, cats walkin like they in a Western even though they livin in the city, they walk that walk and look like they ain't never gonna let nobody bug them ... and they got them fine good-quality guns stuck down in they belts. That's what I call a movie, Jack!

Sometime my mama and Butler almost be like a real movie, they laugh and hurry out the door like they got some wild, crazy secret and like everybody else is out of it, you know? She wear them tight, pretty, silky dresses with sequins and beads on the neck and sleeve, and smellin so good with perfume. He fine and neat in his navy blues. When they hit the sidewalk, he's holdin up his hand and whistlin for a taxi like he the King of New York; me and Grandma be lookin out the window all excited cause they done turn us on with their fine way of going out. Grandma say, "Oh, joy! That's what you call happy!" But all of a sudden I'm wonderin in my mind, what they need with me? What they need with Grandma? What they need with anybody? I feel like a accident that happen to people. My blood father cut out on Mama. Musta gone cause he didn't dig me. Mama look at me lotta times and say, "My God, you look just like Big Benny, just like him." Her eyes be sad when she say it. Other times she studyin my face lookin like bout to say somethin, she almost say it, then wave her hand and say, "Never mind." She sayin never mind cause it's me. She don't say that to Butler.

I ask Grandma, "How come Mama gotta be whisperin and talkin secrets in Butler's ear all the time?"

Grandma say, "That's man-woman, and you haven't grown to know bout that yet."

I know I got a real father somewhere, and I bet Butler feelin biggety cause he's here and my real father is gone. I look at Butler quick sometime so I can catch him lookin biggety, but he slick enough to stay cool-lookin.

Sittin in Tiger's pad, I'm latchin onto some heavy thoughts and diggin how smart I really am. I don't care nothin a-tall bout nobody's next move ... not even mine!

After that, some days I went for a hit, other days I didden, was justa off-and-on thing. Sometime, after a score, I'd be wishin there was a school examination test gonna take place cause I felt like it'd be easy to pass—but soon I'd get sleepy and don't care to blow my wig on no questions. Just sittin, feelin nothin, no pain. One day I thought it would be a groove to go by Tiger's and do my second or third mainline, just for a way to pass some time, dig? He got the red stamp up on the downstairs wall, but I go on past that cause now my patience is gettin tired of all this jive bout his aunt and her sleep-in job and all. Either you in somethin or you ain't, right?

I ring the bell and feelin evil when he hassles me bout how I got the wrong place. I don't move a inch cause I ain't one-a his chickens. I say, "Man, gimme some action and no stories." He look at me like he gonna go up side my head, but somethin told him to cool it.

He slip me a name and address and tell me, "Just say 'Tiger and Kenny—they my boons.' Thass our secret, okay?"

The address turn out to be a candy store, but ain't no fellow name Walter there, just a old guy wipin off the counter with a dirty rag. I say, "Where is Walter?" Old guy look mad when he hear me say that.

"Git out," old man say. "Walter might be on the sidewalk, but he ain't inside-a here. Got it?" I got outside and stand.

Then this skinny, lean cat come over from cross

the street. "You lookin for somebody round here?" he ask.

I fall in with the high sign. "Tiger and Kenny, they my boons."

He laugh, "Where's your diaper?"

I flash the color of my money and say, "Cool me, that's what." He went in the candy store with me followin behind. Cooled me in the back room. The old guy still moppin the counter, but he lookin scared like the worst chicken in the world.

"You more man than Tiger and Kenny put together." Walter lookin satisfy with me, he say, "Bring me some cash-in-advance customers, and I'll treat you right bout whatever you need ... bring cash and you'll get yours, plus you won't ever be broke."

So that gave me two places to go, and that's how it is, one place leads to another, and soon you can score anytime you wanta. You can walk up to a stranger and say, "My old man gotta score, or he gonna kill me." If you picked the wrong cat, he don't know what you talkin bout or will say, "Get outta my face!" But if you picked the right one, he'll take your bills and leave your stuff on a garbage can cover or drop it behind a old box that might be sittin there. They don't wanta be seen layin nothin in your hand. Ain't no trouble to find skag. So how can I say who did what and who is sellin? Right is right, I got some honor. Not like my main boon who cut out on me after we first lighted up together.

One time I say to Jimmy-Lee, "Hey, my man, let's go somewhere and smoke us a joint."

He say, "Man, I got somethin else for a dollar to do." Sure, when he was smokin, I smoked with him; then after I start, he quit. But that's OK, later for phonies! Meanwhile, back at the ranch, what's my stepfather doin? He drinkin his mash and talkin civil rights trash, like what all he could do if he was President of the U.S. of A. The nigga ain't nothin but a maintenance man! My mama busy makin him ham and egg sandwiches serve with cold beer. Grandma stompin her feet, singin "Near-o My God." Act like God is her chum-buddy. If God dig her so hard, how come she havin a tough time like everybody else? She keep sayin, "Pray, Benjie, pray for what you want." Later for the phonies! They all do some fool think but want me perfect.

Now I'm layin up in this hospital bed tryin to keep my wits sharp so's not to put the whole neighborhood in jail by rattin on em when I get ast questions. This Black doctor wearin a white coat like a short-order cook, he comin round with the nurse, servin medicine. They also givin vitamin pills and shots in the butt, and I'm drinkin down glasses of funny-tastin stuff. Doctor try to act like a boon soul. I say, "What is this I gotta take?"

And he say, "Do you question the street dealer when he sells you a deck of horse mix with talcum?"

I look him in the eye and drink the medicine. Fellas in other beds watchin, so I say, "My mama never had no chickens."

Doc laugh and pinch my cheek so hard he almost draw blood. He say, "That's trankalizer." He lookin at me like ready to cry. I can't stand nobody treatin me like pitiful, I rather be kill, thassa fact.

I'm feelin sleepy. The nurse givin butt shots. She say it's iron and vitamins. I'm sleepy too much. Wakin up and seein folk laughin while layin in their beds. My stomach sickly from trankalizer and vitamins ... I'm tired and sad, feelin sometime hot and sometime cold. I wish I had me one friend, one who dig me the most and don't put anybody else ahead of me. Guess I'm in this sad world all by myself. Nobody care, why should they if your own daddy run off? They don't mean no harm, they can't help it. Trouble is this, too many folks expeck other folks to be carin bout them when it ain't noway possible. So I'm laying here learnin how to expeck nothin. My toes, ankles, and legs look skinny and ashy dark. A narrow-face, yaller-headed white boy is in the bed cross the way, lookin at me like he wanta say somethin, but he waitin for me to be the one to speak first. I ain't gonna ast him shit. He don't go to my school and don't live round here. Layin in our hospital, he oughta speak first. I been through the hot and cold shivers, the head shrinks, and the visitor hour, so damn if I'm gonna make over him and be astin things. How come he can't ast me? Everybody always waitin to see where I'm comin from. I don't feel like before skag and don't feel skagged ... feel old and beat, feelin jumpy and scared. I don't know what I'm scared of. I don't like bein a scared-a nothin. My mama didn't have no chickens, you know.

BENJIE JOHNSON

At home now for a week. They got my room fix up with a new bedspread and curtains. Bedspread got green rabbits on it, curtains just plain blue with nothin. I'm too old for rabbits, but blue curtains look groovy. House now quieter than ever before. Everybody polite to each other and tiptoein round. We got two kindsa ice cream, also fruit and cookies in the house. All talkin to me like I'm some stranger from outer space. "You really lookin fine." They keep sayin it. Grandma look at me and wag her finger. "You a *good* boy, Benjie, just good as can be." I don't wanta talk. I'm tryin to think how to do better and do what the soul doctor say: "Start anew, son." He's not the worst person in the world, you know.

I told him, "I don't do nothin right in the first place much less doin it *anew*."

"The world ain't perfect," Soul doctor say. "But hard as it is, life is still sweet. Dig life. That's why I'm a doctor, because I dig life."

My so-call stepfather, Butler, come in the room to have one-a them draggy heart-to-hearts. He tellin me how buddies is suppose to stick close to each other and tell and confide. All of a sudden my mama standin in the doorway listenin to how it's all goin down, so I move in and take over and say,

75

"Relax, pal, you just a maintenance man—and we livin in a time when a hero ain't nothin but a sandwich—so don't strain yourself tryin to prove nothin." Butler turn round and ast Mama, "You wanta go over to the Paradise Bar for a cold brew so I can clear this boy outta my head?"

She say, "I'll go with you." When she talk to him, her voice rise up higher like she gonna sing a song. Mama act like Butler's Uncle Tom.

When they gone, I come out in the livin room and Grandma sittin there. "Boy, you all right?" she ast. I try to think up a serious thing to say that might be interestin to a old person. "Why is it," I ast, "that yall got bunnies on my bedspread but the curtains just plain? I like plain the best."

She snap me up somethin terrible, "Because," she say, "material *with* bunnies was three for a dollar and plain cost seventy-five cents a yard!" You can't be sociable with her. Then she holler bout how God knows she did her best when she use her "poor old hands" to make me bedspread and curtains. Ran in her room and slam the door, then lock it. Yeah, got a lock put on her door while I was in the hospital.

They can have back the spread and curtains, I'm too old for them fuckin bunnies anyway. I went in the bathroom, got down on the cold tile floor and prayed like never before in life, didn't pray no "Now I lay me down" like when I was a chile. "Please, God," I prayed, "send me a friend, someone to be crazy bout *me*. Pleeeeease, God " I wait for like how Grandma say she get a *sign*. Nothin happenin but the sounda the faucet leakin. God somewhere else. I hit the bathtub so hard almost broke my hand.

I search for money. Ain't nothin in Mama's drawer, or the kitchen, or the bathroom, or anyplace. I open the closet door, and there is Butler's best suit and overcoat. I'm not gonna go on skag again, but I'm gonna main it one more time ... so I'll remember what I'm givin up. I kicked once and I can kick anytime I wanta. Butler deserve to be punish, and she do too. He *livin* with my mama and makin out like he care bout me. They ain't ast me what I think bout them livin together. If she wanta live with somebody, why I gotta live with em too? If she separate from somebody, why I gotta separate? Bein a chile is bein a slave, and that's why I'm glad I ain't a chile no more. I'm takin his clothes; after all, he's takin my mama. Somebody who need the coat can use it, it'll do em some sincere good, and they'll gimmie a few dollars for myself. Damn, I ain't the worst person in the world.

One time I deliver some skag for Walter, and when I bring him his money back, he give me a light fix for free. I don't believe in stealin, but my mama would sure rather I take Butler's things than go round pushin for Walter. Anyway, whatever anybody rather, I ain't never comin back. My real daddy don't want me and I'm damn sick and tireda havin Butler strainin to make out like he digs me and I'm his boon. It ain't true! It phony everywhere!

MISS EMMA DUDLEY

Neighbor

DEAR SISTER CLARA,

Hope these few words find you well. How is North Carolina these days? This neighborhood is getting closer to hell by the minute. I would gladly move back down home like you asked, but there is something about all that quiet that just seems to get to me. I have put out the word to try and get me a reliable male roomer, for the sake of income and protection. Me and my dog ain't enough. Woofie makes noise but thieves no longer fear dogs. I can't advertise in the newspaper for a roomer. I read about a woman takin in a stranger who went basurp in the middle of the night and whacked her with a hatchet. She didn't die, but she'll never be the same.

I have to be careful who comes in my house, I'm still an attractive woman looking twenty years younger than my neighbors, but most of them got some kind of man and I haven't. Men are blind and don't know beauty and virtue when they see it. There's a fine-looking man living upstairs in this same apartment house ... nicely built, hardworking, and carries himself with a manly air. Name is Butler Craig. Wouldn't you know he let himself get attached to a dumpy, plain woman they call Sweets. She's got a son named Benjie who is a thirteen-year-old junkie. Butler Craig always asks me about North Carolina because I once told him we have a family farm. I'd move back down home if I had a husband to keep me from bein lonely. Pray I get a man like this Butler.

LOVE,
YOUR SISTER EMMA

BUTLER CRAIG

Livin in the same house, but had to move downstairs. Miss Emma Dudley was nice enough to rent me space, and I do appreciate it, because she usually doesn't rent to people and I don't blame her. If I had a fine, quiet apartment to myself, I wouldn't rent out a room to a livin. There's somethin to be said for wakin up in the mornin all by yourself. You hear lotta blues songs bout bein lonesome; bet they weren't written by somebody who had to live boxed up with other people. It's also nice to wake up knowin that if you hung your overcoat in the closet last night, then it gotta still be hangin there this mornin; at least if it's gone, it had to be taken by somebody who broke in, and not by somebody who's livin there.

Miss Emma Dudley's got a police dog that'll bark you outta your head when you come near the front door. I had to get used to that.

"Don't pay him no mind, Mr. Butler," she say. "He just showin off. His bark is worse than his bite."

When somebody ring the bell, that dog, Woofie, runs down the length of the hall and throws hisself against the door like as if to break right on through it. I really had to get used to that.

Miss Emma Dudley came to my room door

wearin a long pink, silk dress, the front cut down so low till look like any minute her knockers was gonna pop out and sing Glory Hallelujah. She's bringin a bottle of scotch, two glasses, and some snacks on a tray.

"Like to calm your nerves?" she say.

I didn't know what to answer, and before I could think up somethin, she's sittin on the foota my bed pourin drinks.

"I got a lovely, thick T-bone steak, if you're up to it," she say.

She goes chattin on bout this and that and how good her job is and bout the pension it will someday pay, smoothin her hands over her bosoms and pattin them back down in place, so they won't tumble over the fronta her dress.

Truth be known, I do feel like eatin a T-bone steak, and also gettin a little interested in anything else she might think up, but warnin signals are goin through my mind. You hear women complainin how they hate to go to dinner with a guy who's expectin some immediate return on his investment, but you don't hear bout the men who have eaten some woman's home cookin, and she's sittin there expectin him to, at least, marry her. Of course, in this case, there's more than cookin bein offered and advertised. Her charms are definitely on display, she's crossed her legs and hiked the pink dress up to her thigh, showin black stockins look like made out of lace. And I see she has long, furry eyelashes on ... and battin them up and down while talkin. When she's laughin, she hold her head back and her mouth wide open, the overhead light is throwin 75 watts on her back, gold teeth. Miss Emma Dudley is a fine, flashy-lookin woman.

Bein by myself has its drawbacks. I miss Sweets.

I feel like a fool goin up to see her whenever Benjie is out of the way, but I can't trust myself to face him. After me goin to school, seein teachers, psychiatrists, the police; after havin heart-to-hearts with him, to think he would rob me of my suit and overcoat. When he was in the hospital for detox, he said, "Don't nobody believe in me, Butler. If somebody believe in me, I swear I could do just fine. But nobody in the world believe in me no kinda way, bout nothin."

He was lookin so downhearted and sad. I felt sorry for him, *more* than sorry because his Grandma was goin on through visitin hour like she never gonna stop.

"A criminal, a thirteen-year-old, dope-fiend criminal. He's headin for the jailhouse. He stole my three dollars, and yall upheld him in it. It was mine, so yall didn't care that much!"

Everybody gets so excited until each talk turns into a ruckus. The social worker said to "discuss" together, didn't say to shout and accuse. What makes me mad is how we all get excited while Benjie sits there the coolest one. He asked to have somebody believe in him, so I went for it. When he came home, first thing I said was, "We gonna believe in you, son, you and me gonna be buddies through this, gonna be close together and come out winners."

All shook hands with each other, and each pledged how much each would do. Sweets' mama promised not to be pickin and naggin, and I promised to spend my free time with him to help beat temptation. I also gave the little double crosser the telephone number on my job, so he could call me in case he needed somebody real fast. Benjie had got to me so until I was fightin back tears, almost boohooin out loud. Even went in the kitchen and made the son-bitch a milk shake with a egg in it. Was a feelin in the air like we had it made and was on the right track. Sweets' mama busied around doin nice things, brushin off his school jacket and sprinklin his sport shirt to iron it. We had it made. Sweets' mama say, "This feel like a true Christian home this evenin, really do." Once in a while you can have a perfect minute, a hot spot of time when you can say ... that went well, proud of myself. It was like that for us, and he blew it again.

How much understandin can you have? I ain't God. If it's Sweets' fault or mine, all we can do is try ... and I did that. She's still doin it, but I've had it. I knew it was time to get my hat before I lost control and killed the hard-headed junkie. Thirteen and forty-three ain't no match for each other. If I lay my hands on him, he'll be dead. I'm wore out from dealin with Benjie and holdin down a hardworkin job at the same time. I punch a time clock at seven every mornin, so that means rise and shine by five. I can't be stayin up till one A.M. beggin a boy to behave. My head is so full of Benjie till my mouth runs off to Miss Emma Dudley.

"Miss Emma," I say, "would your family down South be interested in boardin Sweets' boy for a few months? I'd pay them fair and meet the payment regular so he could be away from the city and able to see sky and run and play where there's no concrete and crowds. Me and Sweets could breathe easy for a while and maybe patch differences the child has made between us ..." I stop when I see Miss Emma Dudley's eyes turn cold and harder than the ice in her glass.

She smoothed her bosoms, then picked up her tray of scotch and goodies. "I'm confused, Mr. Butler," she say, "there must be some kind of misunderstanding. I'm looking for ways to improve *my* life, not Sweets'. Why should my relatives take in her trouble?" She lean over close to my face and whisper, "Think about it, Mr. Butler, maybe you need to burn a few bridges behind you and find yourself a woman who's more your kind. Somebody could make you a good wife." With that she flounces on out. Guess she told me.

JIMMY-LEE POWELL

Benjie's Friend

I'm passin my test papers and goin ahead of everybody else in track and basketball. I also got me a Saturday job at the grocery store. One time Benjie say to me, "Man, you got it made!"

I rock back on my heels lookin wise, fakin like I know some secret thing he ain't in on, then I say, "Just hangin in there, man, that's all." People like you to be actin cool and powerful, like you a real heavy person, in charge of your situation at all times. I ain't really got it all together. But soon as my bread piles up, I'm gonna get me a set-a drums and learn how to play em, that's bout the only secret I got.

Fact is, if I was on skag or just out of jail, they would maybe buy me a set-a drums just to help me straighten up. Sure, if I was in a drug bag, they'd pay me money to go to school and give me a head shrinker too. Some cats come outta detention and soon have folks advisin and workin to help them make it big. I'd like a little help myself, but I don't wanta get in trouble to get it, not really. I wish there was some place to go without bein in trouble.

I'd go to that place, ring the bell, and say, "Please let me stay here until I get myself together. I'm not in trouble and my parents doin the best they can, but I don't wanta be home." Grown people got this deal where they get divorced from each other. The father and mother explain to the kid how they gonna divorce, but that it has nothin to do with the kid because the parents respectin and lovin him right on. Well, why can't you divorce your relatives?

I wanta get out from home. I could go to a place called "skag" and shoot up till there's nothin on my mind a-tall, but that's a trip you soon gotta take every day and, somewhere long the line, I'd get sicka catchin the same old train, but then it might be too late to get off.

I dig a place where somebody will open the door when you knock. They'd say, "Come on in. How's everything? What can I do for you?"

I'd say, "Nobody did no big wrong to me, but I gotta get a divorce from my parents, my neighborhood, my school, and my old buddies, so I can think or not think for two-three weeks. Could I come in without a habit or bein in bad with the law?"

The one who answer say, "That's what this place is for. We dig." He would call my home telephone and then say, "Hey, yall, Jimmy-Lee is here with us. He sends his best and say tell you he's just takin a divorce for now. . . . So yall go on to sleep, Jimmy-Lee is fine."

He'd show me to my private room and say, "Rest yourself, maybe in a day-so you might wanta rap on somethin." I'd stay there till I was together enough to go home again, or go wherever. Sure, they'd help anybody even if they didden snatch a pocketbook or shoot up.

I'd tell Benjie bout it, and he could go divorce trouble steada divorcin me, who was his boon.

Nigeria Greene would be a good one for the door opener in a place like that.

Benjie don't half bother to speak to me anymore. If I was in trouble, like him, we would still be buddies. Friendship begin to split when one is caught in a habit and the other not. I've seen it time and time, needles divide guys, because the user rather be round another junkie. He through with you because he thinkin you lookin down on him. You through with him because you get scared of him, he smells like trouble when the monkey rides his back. Soon he's got to hustle hard for the monkey, and he hangs out with nobody but other hard hustlers.

...

BENJIE JOHNSON

This counselor think he slick. He actin cool and
maybe talk bout baseball or bout how he dig jazz;
he lookin up in the air or down at the ground, to
sneak up on makin me talk bout myself. Is all right
with me cause he's a social worker and thass how
they taught to do, but it gets me in the gut how he
be actin like he really care. They all belong to the
same club—Nigeria, Cohen, counselor, Butler, all of
'em. You'd think they dig me more than they do
theyself. They just puttin on this buddy stuff cause
they don't want me givin them and the society a
lotta bother. Nobody digs a junkie, not that I'm one
but they be thinkin I am, so it's most the same
thing. Nobody digs niggas either, not even other
niggas. White folks don't want you livin near them,
and Black always preachin at your ass bout how
you got no pride in yourself and your history. One
good thing Jimmy-Lee's father once said, "Our history is dead if all it got to show is how we once
could speak another language. History is to be
made very day, not just told from some long time
ago."

This counselor, I know the only reason we goin
for a walk and talk is cause he gets paid to do it. If
not for cats like me, his behind would starve to
death. Sometime I *wanta* talk to him, but I don't

88

like to rap bout my mother and relatives and bout
underprivilege. Not that Hank be sayin "low-socio"
and words like that. He's white but also a little bit
smart and too slick for that. I gotta watch real
sharp to see he don't catch me off-base. If I'm not
careful, I might spill my guts. If they wanta talk me
outta fixin, they should just do that. But Hank be
tryin to find out how I started. He say, "You're a
guy with a good brain, how'd you get into this?" I
do wanta at least get along with Hank's program,
give him things to put down on his report paper,
help him out so we both be lookin good and pleasin
everybody. After all, the man gotta hold his job. I
know, I don't *have* to be usin, it's somethin I started, but not a habit. I'd be a fool not to dig when
skag is gettin to me. If that happen, I'll really stop.

Hank be waitin to hear bout my discontent with
life and droppin hints for me, dig? So I follow up
on what we drop. I'm sayin how nobody understand
me, my school work ain't comin long so hot, not got
the clothes I want for school, and like that. He be
actin understandin, puttin his arm round my shoulder like boons forever. I know he ain't my boon and
I'm not his. He live as far off from me as his white
ass can get. No matter how many stories he tell
bout baseball players and boxers who come out the
slums, I notice he ain't movin in here so his son can
get the chance to be a great athlete. People think
you a fool.

I do my rappin on the inside, I rap to myself. I
have got high and done some rappin with Kenny,
but even then I'm holdin back, dig? People always
gotta prove how you wrong and not seein the true
picture. They don't know *my* true picture. If you do
tell your truth, they will work on you till you take
it back and say you wrong.

I know what my picture is. I hate school, even feel bad walkin to the school, forcin my feet to move where they don't wanta go. Schoolteachers can be some hard-eyed people, with talkin eyes; they mouth sayin one thing and them eyes be screamin another. Teach will say, "Be seated and open your book to page one nineteen and be prepared to read as I call your name." But them eyes be stonyin down on you, speakin the message: "Shits, sit your ass down, open the book, and make a fool outta your dumb self when I start calling on the ones who the poorest readers."

Thass the message coming at you from whiteys. Then you got the special look that comes by short-wave from Black ... they lookin sad like they could bust inta tears and they be sighin and shakin heads while they eyes sayin, "My people, my people, yall some bad-luck, sad-ass niggas." Then there a few like Nigeria Greene, he lookin at you all bright-eyed-Black and tellin how we descend from kings and queens back in Africa, how we was great when whitey was still a caveman in Europe. But like Jimmy-Lee's father say, "Trouble is, we got no kings and queens right this very minute, and we ain't found out how to deal with that." I iced on Nigeria when he teamed up with Cohen and turned me in. That don't sound like descend from kings and queens, do it? He oughta take that green, red, and black button off his bespoke suit. And that Bernard Cohen be sayin the wrong thing every time he open his mouth. He say, "You can be somebody if you want." How the shit he don't know I'm somebody right now? He think *he* somebody and I'm not. He sincere, and I say ... Hooray for sincere! ... but it don't buy no steaks or pleat-back suits. His face look like a stompin ground for sadness

when he be talkin serious and usin words like
"ghetto." Now, since he and Nigeria got so close
they can piss through a straw together, they sayin
"inner city." Inner city ain't nothin but the place
they useta call ghetto and slum, dig?

I hate cafeteria in school. They got a steam table
that'll blow your cool. They cook shiny, big garbage
cans fulla soup. Cafeteria help be ploppin long-han-
dled dippers and spoons down in brown, muddy
gallonsa soup, stirrin and diggin up beans and car-
rots, splashin it out in your bowl like you a dead-
ass nuisance that keep on needin to eat all time.
They be sayin, "Speak up, bread or roll!" and "Step
lively, move on!" They oughta put that message on
a eight-track tape so they can shut up and just dip.

If I was to pick out middle C on the piano and
keep hittin it, thass how it sound when my jography teacher be teachin. I don't listen, just turn her
off and stare out the window at sky and freedom,
thinkin how it would be if I had finish servin my
time and was gone from here with my diploma ...
or gone without it. Then I'm hearin middle C get
louder on my ear, she astin me to repeat what she
been sayin. I wanna say, "Bitch, I'm tryin not to
hear you." But since I got a mother, I'm thinkin
jography teacher might be somebody's mother too,
so I say, "I didden hear the last part."

Look like she could be decent and repeat it, but
she wanta outfox you, so she say, "Tell us what
part you did hear." When you don't answer, she
flippin through her report book to make another
mark gainst your record. I hate school, and that's
how come I got to cuttin class and hangin out with
those who hate the same.

Maybe it's like Butler say before he moved out
on us, "Boy, you hate everybody, the whole coun-

try and all what's in it." Now that Butler's downstairs to Miss Emma Dudley's, I'm hatin him more than school or the society. He made my mother cry. "You got him!" he told her. "Can't be both me and your son. I can't live with a lyin, thievin junkie! He's your blood, so there's no way to ask you to give him up. You got him, he's all yours!"

Mama say, "Yes, he's mine, and I'm his." She really standin up for me but cryin so hard like she can never stop.

Grandma was the one who surprise me, she beg Butler not to go. Damn, more than one time I heard her say, "Sure hadn't counted on him makin this his full-time home." Now she turn round and say, "Please, Butler, don't leave us!" Grabbin at his jacket and tryin to pull him back.

Mama say, "*Let* him go!"

Butler look sheepy and say, "Hell. I ain't goin nowhere but downstairs to Miss Emma Dudley. Call if you need me." I hate him more than ever. He's gone, but Mama and Grandma still talkin bout him and wishin he was back.

Newspaper advertisement:

REMOVE ALL EVIL

Do you need help? Mme. Snowson is in town with African secrets from the Deep South. I am a reader and adviser with answers. You don't tell me, I tell you. There is a cure for every problem. Evil spells have been removed after one visit. I give you, free of charge, one capsule of anointing oil, a ceremonial African incense stick, and a trial package of South Carolina Herbal Tea. These gifts are yours to keep as a special blessing. Enemies can be vanquished while you wait. You can have peace of mind by tomorrow sunrise. Has your loved one gone? Divine power and know-how can bring about a return. Know this! When everything goes wrong . . . something evil is working against you! Study the following testimonials:

"I have been blessed with money, love, and a fine house."

J. Smith, Newark, N.J.

"God bless you, Mme. Snowson! I am well and have won $500."

B. Monroe, Baltimore, Md.

"Have just married the lady of my choice and own two cars. Every blessing is now ours. My health so improved that operation is no longer necessary. I am sending money for the large size oil and more incense and tea. Thank you for being my way-shower."

R. Robinson, Los Angeles, Calif.

MADAM SNOWSON IS OPEN SEVEN DAYS A WEEK
NOON TO MIDNIGHT
CALL . . . 558-67 . . . .

MRS. ROSE JOHNSON (CRAIG)

Benjie's Mother

Mama talked me into goin for a readin and a blessin, but she couldn't have if there wasn't somethin inside drivin me on to do it. I don't believe in fortune-tellers, but I believe in Benjie, so that's what sent me to Madam Snowson's.

We had to wait our turn in a small room while the reader told fortune in what they call "the consultation parlor." There were two before us. An old woman who kept rockin back and forth, and another lady busy drummin her fingers on the arms of her chair.

Mama whispered, "Alla this is gettin to my nerves." My mind stayed on Benjie and Butler.

The place smelled like fried liver and onions. It wasn't a bad smell, just a perfumy odor like what comes from good, fresh food when somebody knows how to cook it, however ... I don't too much care for onions myself.

When the assistant, a young, pretty girl with a fluffy Afro hairdo, opened the consultation parlor door, to let a customer out, a trail of incense floated in behind her. I felt kinda tight inside like when you visit the doctor or dentist. One time we heard a customer cry out from the inner room, "Yes, yes, indeed! That's right!" Some say women are not able to keep a secret, but this is one happenin Butler will never know bout from me. I'd never hear the end of it. Anyway, now that he's moved downstairs to Miss Emma Dudley's, he doesn't need to hear of each and every thing I do. If he was at home, maybe I wouldn't be here tryin to find another way to save Benjie.

The assistant did not want us both in at the same time. "It's gonna cost yall five apiece anyway, so each may's well get the full separate treatment." I handed her a ten-dollar bill and told her we weren't tryin to do the reader out of her rightful fee. We went in together. The parlor was dark, lit only by a dim lamp with a reddish shade and several candles throwin large, fluttery shadows on the wall. The incense smoke and smell was heavy. I felt dizzy.

The reader is a skinny, short dark lady. She wears a plain blue smock and a fancy silver cross hangin from a chain. She has a goiter or some kinda growth in her neck, her eyes are wide open and stary. The room is skimpy on furniture, but me and Mama sit down on the best piece, a gold brocade-satin couch which is protected by a see-through plastic cover. The reader is silent as a grave in her straight-back chair; a small table is next to it; on the table is a fishbowl filled with water.

Madam dips her hands in the bowl; the assistant gives her a lacy towel. She dries her drippin fingers. We can hear water drops hitting the floor ... plip, plip, plip.

"Ohhhhhhhh," Madam leans back and groans, "yall comin to me with such a heavy burden, it takes two to bear it. Bringin trouble like that cross which Jesus dragged to the killin place. Ohhhhhh, what a weight to bear."

Mama starts cryin. I take her arm and squeeze hard so she'll get back control.

Madam whispers, "Lord Lord, Lord, tell us how to untangle Satan's bloody, meddlin horns from these troubled heart strings!"

I hear the outside swish of city traffic, the faraway happy sound of children laughin and playin somewhere down the street. My fingernails clutch into the palms of my hands, I'm prayin hard for help. I whisper the word to Madam: "Dope, my sister, the trouble is dope. Dope is takin away my son and my man . . . I want both of 'em back."

"Well, Lord," she says, "you hearin from us again. Ain't you gonna give us credit for faith? We the most faithful people you ever made and not even in your own likeness. I know you gonna lead us beside the still water and restore our soul . . . in the long run. But, we need you right now, Lord—let dope dealers die from the hurtin they puttin on us! Let our poor children seal their veins against the attack of Satan's needles! Wash us strong and healthy! Wash us on a foamy, clean tide which will safely float us up to higher ground. Give us joy in the promise of evil defeated! Let this woman again see your love shinin in her man's eyes. Remember your promise, Lord! Deliver us from evil!"

I gave the reader a extra three dollars for a bottle of Indigo Blue. Free of charge, she gave me holy water to sprinkle in the corners of my apartment, to chase away evil. I'm to take a warm bath colored with Indigo Blue. I'm gonna lay down in blue water and give magic power a chance to wash off my hard luck. I don't want my son to die.

NIGERIA GREENE

Me and my wife paid twenty-five dollars a ticket to honor a Negro writer-rascal last night. Yeah, he was a rascal, a rogue, a thief, and a forked-tongue put-downer of everything Black that ever lived and breathed bad air.

Every time he hits a lick at his typewriter he carries us one step further away from freedom. We sat there spellbound, wearin painted-on grins ... along with our tuxedos and dashikis, yeah, in uniform to honor a rascal.

The guest of honor read from his book, preachin how all that ever held us back was mama, sister, girlfriend and ... "the vast majority of misguided sisters and brothers!" We were rockin with laughter, but in the middle of a big ha-ha, a sick feelin hits me in the gut ... I realize my stomach resents what my brain is acceptin.

I look around see nothin but Black fat cats, those of us who have recently resigned from the house and field nigga society ... we're fulla eats and twelve-year-old likker, we're now shinier than a pre-Civil War slave used to get on catfish fried in saturated hot grease. When this rascal finishes tellin us how the race is nothin, the whole room rises and we give him a Black standin ovation. Dig it, I find

myself makin hooray noise right along with the
rest.

We so-called "high achievers"—doctors, lawyers,
teachers, actors, painters, poets, dancers—most of
us now makin a buck offa either "puttin down the
nigga" or "upliftin the nigga" on some specially
"funded" gigs ... we're the upper-strata welfare
recipients, dig? Old slave massa's computer-pro-
grammed son has figured out a new category for us.
While we were busy evaluatin "the house and field
nigga," he came up with "the funded nigga" ...
those of us runnin round talking trash and drinkin
our mash outta long-stem champagne glasses handed to us by smirkin time-and-a-half white waiters.

We got some special type guest white folk, too,
they laughin louder than anyone else at the whitey
jokes, they also enjoyin their newfound freedom of
callin us "nigga" out loud, to our face, which deed
is suppose to show that ain't nobody sensitive anymore, specially us. Fact is, we have turned into the
most *in*sensitive bunch you'll find anywhere west of
hell. There's also a light smatterin of Blacks who
work hard for a livin, from pushin dress racks to
makin change in the subway. This is their night to
"pass" as professionals, they are for the evening
"in" dress designing, or business programming,
counseling, "urban" projects and a great many ini-
tialed endeavors whose initials spell out words ...
SCRAM, SCOOT, FITE, GONE, and so on.

The MC is glad-greetin everybody and handin
out compliments two for a penny, as usual, givin his
all no matter what the cause or the purpose. The
cat next to me whispers, "Say he gets up every
mornin and turns on the news to see which way the
wind is blowin, before he answers his telephone.
After all, gotta know which bag to jump in, right?"

The platform is full of funded celebrities and fund raisers, big-time little spenders ... to keep the ghetto cool, as well as Black and beautiful. Within the past twelve months they have all taken positions against school busin and comin on strong as the hallelujah chorus with a new name for segregation; "QUALITY EDUCATION" ... which is where the struggle is safer and about to be funded and refunded for the next many years.

Here and there are a few wistful, bewildered, lost, lonely let-down brothers and sisters who are now beginnin to feel somethin must be wrong with themselves because they have let this hustler's harvest pass. The intellectual poor, those who have never been met at an airport by an air-conditioned chauffeured limousine, those who never heard the mayor speak at a midday luncheon, those never called to a White House conference, those not on casual speakin terms with the State Department.

The evening drank itself to an end when the liquor ran out along with the salted peanuts. The upper crust "in" group went off to the Top of the Sevens for "gin and ginger" with their white boons, the fringe-benefit-almost-in group went off to a pot-smoke-and-chili party to rap the guest of honor over the righteous coals. The guest of honor, "they" say, went off to meet a once-was-an-almost-top-white-movie-star, to snuggle against her boobs and cuss all other niggas till the dawn of another new day.

Me and my socializin African queen cabbed back uptown, with a few other tolerated squares, tryin to talk ourselves into likin what we've been doin, but bein and feelin less like ourselves, less and less. Now, in the calm of the mornin after, I'm askin myself what else is there? With a splittin headache,

I'm facin my fate as a plain, uninfluential grade school teacher ... knowin there are some Black children to be met, knowin there's nothin heard last night that can be passed on to them with pride. If they are shootin shit in the arm, their elders are shoutin shit in the head ... but we *never* OD out. Benjie killers! Laughin Benjie on to early death; drinkin his blood from a champagne glass. We're in some terrible trouble, but the kids don't need any more tired, opportunistic advice.

I'm gonna stand up tomorrow and tell my class, "Under adult supervision you have become a breed of junkies and acid trippers, muggers, purse snatchers and trust-no-one-over-thirtyites. You right not to trust anyone over thirty, we're makin millions outta your slave bodies, makin big profit from openin your veins and making small profit trying to close them shut again. Yall better learn to defend yourself."

Junkie, junkie, you pushin horse to yourself. The latest war is goin on within the confines of your very own veins ... and so far the nation is losin. ...

BENJIE JOHNSON

I been bathin my own self for years, for as long as I can recall, so I don't dig Mama givin me a bath in blue water. That's the most humiliatinest thing that ever happen. She pour blue dye in the bath water and say, "Hop in there, I'm gonna sponge you all over."

"For what?" I ast.

"To wash all the devil and hell off you."

"Ain't no devil and hell on me."

She pullin at my shirt and unbucklin my belt. She strong, Jack! She strong like crazy and pullin at my clothes so bad, till I say, "Awright, I'll take 'em off by myself!" She stop and stand back with her hands on her hips, still fussin.

"You better! I don't believe in spells; but if you got one on you, we gonna wash it off tonight!"

When you thirteen, you ain't supposed to be buck naked before your mama. I'm holdin a towel in fronta me to cover my personals and try to show respeck; she snatchin the towel off and pushin me in the tub.

"I don't wanta get in it." I say, How I know what that blue water is? How I know it won't gimmie a infection?

Mama curse and say, "Goddammit, you put anything in your arm that some scroungy stranger

101

hand you. You gonna sit the hell on down in this blue water and see what it can do for you."

Mama don't curse, she really don't, will say dammit and what-the-hell, but when she sayin goddammit, that's somethin else. I tried to run out the bathroom. Grabbin the brush she clean the toilet with, she say, "I'll bust your brains loose!" I jump on in the tub fore she lose her mind. She don't leave nothin to do but follow what she say or fight her, so I went sloshin inta the tub. When it splash, she say, "Don'tcha get my hair fulla water! Be still, dammit!"

She's all outta line, but I'm tryin to forgive, cause I know she mad cause Butler is gone and she be missin him. My mama is over thirty-three years old and going on like this bout some man. Maybe she can't help bein old and lovin somebody, but look like a old woman would be satisfy just to be cool and be somebody's mother.

She grab the washcloth and scrub all over me with blue water, my head, neck, it's all in my eyes even, then washin under my arms. "Stand up!" she holler. She washin between my legs and backside, till tears most come to my eyes. Not cause it's hurtin, but cause she's makin me feel shame. She say, "You ain't got nothin down there that I ain't seen before, ain't enough to see noway." Grown people think they can do you like a dog cause they got a few years on you. Ain't no easy way to get along with your relatives. When she think we had a good talk, it's a time when I been sayin, yeah, yeah, yeah, like after the blue bath when she say, "Benjie, you oughta do some better."

"Yeah, I do try."

"You lyin. I don't like that."

"Yeah, yes'm."

"That's better. Somethin on your mind bout me and Butler?"

"I'm glad he's gone away."

"We had planned to be married, but everything is so distress now that I'm not sure it's for the best. Why'd you steal his clothes, Benjie?"

I feel sorry for her cause she ready to cry. She wearin a long housecoat with flowers on it, blue and pink. One thing, she always look nice and neat-lookin. Once, in school, I had to write a composition bout a member of my family, that was when I was young and in lower grade.

Composition went like . . . "My mother is plump but not fat. She is not tall or short, but just in between. She can sew, cook, and clean house nicely. Best thing about her is her walk, goin along like she's on her way to somewhere fine. Thing I don't like the most is her temper. She smile sweet and say, 'Don't do that, honey-bunch,' say it over and over many times real cool, then she snatch up a pillow, throw it at you and yell . . . 'I SAY STOP!' . . . She won't get mad little by little, but just all at once.

"She is very nice-lookin, but not so pretty as to make you feel shame. She has a round face and smooth cheeks with a dimple in one; when she smile, the dimple gets deep. Her color is reddish brown. My grandmother say it is because we got some Indian way back in our family. My mother laugh, show her dimple, and say, 'And a whole lotta African!'

"She is not cheap. She will give me show fare and has also paid for Jimmy-Lee to go with me when his father didden give him fare. She is cool at all times except when very mad."

That's the way the composition went. I won a box of colorin crayons by writin it. Seem a long time

back. Now she cryin. I almost wish Butler would
walk in the door ... almost. Now she take the blue
bottle of dye which a fortune-teller gave her, lookin
at it, laughin and cryin because sometime she can
be sad and tickled at the same time. She pours the
blue down the toilet.

"I know it ain't nothin," she say, "not a damn-ass
thing. Nothin but ignorance and backward as hell."

Jack, if I was a cryin person, I'd cry, too, but I
can't. It would kill me dead for somebody to see me
cry, dig? Tears be burnin and stingin behind my
eyes and like a heavy knot be in my throat. Somethin gotta be done fast, or else I'll cry like a
chicken. Look like my mother dyin of sadness. I
say, "Mama, maybe this blue bath gonna do some
good." She look at me real kind and seem to feel
better. Maybe when I get to be a older man, I'll dig
where she's comin from much better. If I was old,
in Butler's shoes, I might like some nice-lookin
woman myself, even if she did have a son and a
husband who was off somewhere. Life and the society must look different to old people.

BUTLER CRAIG

I feel out of place roomin downstairs here with Miss Emma Dudley, yet wasn't anything to do but leave Sweets. She asked me to come up and have dinner with her last night. I went, but it wasn't the same. The old lady went to mumblin and grumblin, so I just flat-footed asked her what was the matter. She lit into me.

"You mean what the *hell's* the matter! First thing, you can stop callin me 'the old lady'! My name is Mrs. Ransom Bell or else Elizabeth. Always askin Sweets 'How's the old lady?' I'm somebody too, don'tcha know. And stop fixin your voice when you talk to me, fixin it like you talkin to a chile."

That seemed fair enough, to call people what they wanta be called, and in a tone they like. But after I agreed, she still went on.

"Furthermore," she says, "you ran out on Rose. Men are good for nothin but runnin. Some these colored men ain't nothin but breath, britches, and shoe leather! When trouble comes, you run! I told Rosey to keep a sharp eye on the kinda man who runs when trouble comes."

After that, I ran again, made my retreat back down here, and had a night's sleep with peace and quiet. This room is fair-sized and neat, nice curtains at the window. My portable hi-fi is bringin in cool sounds, but through every note all I can think about is Benjie stealin my suit and overcoat. What that old lady—Mrs. Ransom Bell—expect from me? I dead sure can't do a day's work in my socks and underwear. I had to go to the credit place and buy another suit and coat, just in time ... it's snowin and blowin today, Hawkins is really out there. Snow look pretty stickin to the windowpane. This the first quiet day off in the last six weeks, but my mind so tore up till I can't relax. Why should I feel guilty? I didn't harm anybody. When I went upstairs, I put fifty dollars in Sweets' hand so she'd know I'm not really runnin away, no matter what the old lady—Miss Elizabeth—say.

I'm feelin terrible bout bein accused of runnin. If I get hold of Benjie, they'll put me in jail for what they call child batterin. I'll batter on his ass till there's nothin left to hit. How can the boy do somethin terrible, then get mad with me cause I'm the one he did it to? Day before yesterday he crossed to the other side of the street when he saw me comin, actin like he's lookin in store windows. I made a move in his direction, he broke into a run and cut round the corner. Shiiiiit! Boy so damn jealous and mean, he made up his mind not to like me the first time we met.

Social workers, doctors, teachers, all doin what they can and Sweets almost outta her mind! I'm missin her more and more. Damn Benjie Johnson! But a man can't live in a house where he's got no authority! It's Sweets' house and her mama's.

Teacher named Nigeria is okay. He and me went for a beer the time we got Benjie in detox. We see eye to eye except seem like I'm knowin him but he can't know me; however, I won't hold that gainst him because he ain't supposed to know and understand everybody, not even Benjie. His job is to teach kids to study and learn, not how to cut them loose from habits. He kept tellin me that it's nation time, time for us to pull together and rise, work united and all that. I'm agreein, but what good is that, I ain't the one on junk. While we at the bar, drinkin our cold Buds, I pointed out a nodder sittin cross the way, guy half-collapsed over a glassa Coke.

"Too mucha this nation is on the nod," I said.

Nigeria goes rappin on harder than ever. I'm tryin to listen but can't catch hold of anything long enough to turn it over. Cat talks and words tumble outta his mouth, mixed up and leapin from one subject to another, like he gotta tell everything he knows in ten minutes. He keep sayin, "It's nation time!" The cat is strainin so hard to get to me, till I just have to encourage him.

I throw in a "Right on!" when he looks to see what I got to say. I really got nothin to say .. cause I'm busy wonderin how Benjie is handlin the kickin treatment. He was damn lucky to get his butt in that hospital bed. They got a long waitin list, and your people must answer questions and fill out papers. You'd think he wouldn't ever wanta see a fix again. Out less than a week and ripped off my suit. Him bein so young, I thought the cure and our forgiveness would do everything. I was wrong. This Nigeria cat hummed in my ear bout how big-shot whitey gangsters and racketeers are the *real ones* bringin skag into the Black community, and not the street pusher. I say to him, "Man, when they bring it, why we gotta shove it in the nation's arm? Black cats pushin what whitey moves in. If we don't touch it. it'll lay there, right? The Black Nation wanta play blindman's buff and not see these young, hard-ass men out here knockin folks in the head, snatchin pocketbooks, rippin off apartments, shootin down, knifin and muggin. Talk bout pollution in the river and how the fish bein poisoned, dig it, pollution now is in the brain and bloodstream, the very river of life!" No, wasn't nothin he could say back at me, cause right is right.

So now I'm layin here rememberin the past and watchin a snowstorm, feelin the blues. The bell ringin and the mailman is out of the vestibule blowin his screechin whistle. Miss Emma Dudley calls out, "Mr. Butler, mailman got a special delivery letter for me, door is open, but I'll be right back."

"Okay," I say, then turn off the FM. The dog goes runnin out behind her, barkin like the mailman is public enemy number one, I just lay on and think, tryin to figure me and Sweets' problems. A creepy feelin comes over me that I'm not alone. I hear no particular sound that's distinct, but maybe the floor creaked or a draft blew me the message. I know somebody is movin down the long, dark, narrow hall between the front door and the livin room. I've heard bout second sight and how people can know somethin they've not seen or heard, this must be it. All down my spine, in the pit-a my stomach, and at the backa my throat, I'm knowin that Benjie is here. I'm in my pajamas and don't reach for slippers. Barefooted, I get to the door, quietly ease it open and sneak down the hall. The livin room is directly in front of me, and the kitchen is off to the right, just before you reach it.

"Benjie," I say, "you here?"

No answer. I feel kinda silly as I go in the next room. There's a noise behind me. I turn and see him flash outta the kitchen. He's beatin it down the hall, carryin somethin. I light out behind him. "Drop it!" I say. "Drop whatcha got!"

He goes out the front door and takes to the stairs. I'm runnin behind him. Each flight is divided in two, a half flight of steps, then a small landin with a window, a turn and the second part of the flight takes you to the next set of apartments. I think he's headin for home, to Sweets, but on and up he goes past home, to the roof door. I'm puffin and blowin, but gainin ground while he fumbles with the latch on the roof door. He gets the latch off, then has to slam hisself gainst the door. It's jammed. I'm thinkin ... Hot damn! I got him now! All of a sudden he throws his big, shiny somethin at me. I catch it! The son-bitch stole Miss Emma Dudley's electric toaster. I pitch it back at him; but he's gone, and the toaster smashes against the tin door. Somebody on top floor screams. I step out on the roof, into ice and snow; it's wet, cold, and slippery, but I don't give a damn. I want my hands on Benjie. He hops the division leading to the next roof while looking behind to see if I'm closin distance between us.

"You little bastard," I holler, "I'm gonna kill you!"

He zigzags and heads toward the backa the second roof, headin for where the divison leads to a back airshaft; the shaft is an open, straight drop clean down to ground floor. "No," I'm screamin, "not there! Don't do it!" He's on top of the ledge, gonna try to jump the shaft and land on the next roof. He's standin there, slippin, losin his balance. I'm behind him as he slides down and almost straddles the top. I got one arm, he hits and flails out the other and goes over the edge. My hand is grabbed tight around his right arm, just above the elbow. He's swingin down over empty space, lookin up at me, weighin a ton and cryin like crazy. With my other hand I grab his jacket. His face is scared and pinched in like a skinny little old man. The weight of him is growin heavier, feel like holdin a baby grand piano by one leg. He's pullin me down on the wet, icy edge. Can't feel my fingers, have to watch to make sure they don't let loose. Cold as I am, hot sweat breakin out all over. Hands beginnin to sweat, can't tell if it's from Benjie's hand or mine. Wet hands can't hold much longer. He looks down at the courtyard, then up at me, growin heavier and heavier. "Let go, Butler," he says, "let me die. Drom me, man!" He's flailin his legs, tryin to work loose my hold, hollerin and fightin to die. "Let me be dead!"

Feel like I'm standin in a bag-a ice, pullin the shoulder loose from my body. Across my back, behind my knees, shakin and tremblin, gotta let loose ... or go down with him. He keeps sayin it, "Lemme go, man!" I'm scared I'll do it. He's gonna flail around till he solve the problem for me and Sweets. His eyes locked on mine, we lookin right into each other.... Then I know *I was runnin from him* ... like Sweets' mama say. If this was my flesh-and-blood child, I wouldn't have run when he stole my suit ... I went off cause he wasn't mine.

Now I'm inchin him a bit closer, workin and pullin, tryin not to think anymore, but thoughts stay. Benjie has stopped talkin, just hangin, givin up ... given me a chance to kill him. I did want him out of the way, but not dead. I'll die if I lose him! Can't lose him! My knees pressin hard gainst the brick wall, bracin and pullin. His jacket sleeve is tearin, the cheap-Charlie shoulder paddin hangin out. Another strong pull, my arm is twistin outta the raw socket, another pull, my knees gratin gainst bricks, down to the bone.

"Brace yourself," I say, "brace your foot to the wall and climb on up here! Come on! Let's make it!"

He's grabbin to the fronta my pajamas, cloth tearin ... I'm leanin back hard, his head now showin over the edge ... then his chest ... I say, "Come on, goddammit! It's nation time!"

He's squirmin over the top. We fall back on the roof, into the snow, there's blood in the snow, my knees ... bloody from scrapin gainst brick. We sittin there in the cold wet. Benjie's cryin and holdin to me like never gonna let go, body tremblin with the shiverin shakes ... he's cryin the meanness out.

People on the roof shoutin and talkin, Sweets, the man from top floor, Miss Emma Dudley and her big dog, Woofie. Dog runnin back and forth, barkin like Benjie and me make him madder than ever. Miss Emma Dudley holdin up her broke toaster and goin on worse than Woofie. "Don't worry bout no goddamn toaster," I say. "Everything is under control, gonna buy you a new toaster!"

I take Benjie's hand and limp my way down to Sweets' house. I say, "It's you and me from now on, hear?" He still shiverin with a death grip on my hand, his nose and eyes runnin water like Niagara Falls. Sweets look so glad to hear me talkin that way. To myself I'm wonderin what to do beside talk. I don't know what to do. It's a terrible thing not to know what to do.

BENJIE JOHNSON

Butler is cool. I dig how he walks down the street like he ain't to be meddled with; the kinda cat you can call a real man, dig? He might knock you down, or you him, but he'll shake hands when it's all over, that is ... if hand shakin is in order. I also dig him talkin straight to a social worker, a doctor, or even a police. Like when the social worker ast him. "Are you the child's father?" Butler look him in the eye and say, "Let's put it this-a-way. I am who he has *got* for a father, that is sufficient to make him mine and me his."

The social worker look down at his paper, don't know what to write. When he look back up, he figure it's best not to bug Butler, so he say, "I'm gonna put down that you're his stepfather," Butler don't smile or grin but just say, "That'll do."

Hangin by one hand from a roof edge ain't no joke. Lookin down six, seven stories over a concrete backyard will blow your mind if your brain ain't in strong condition. My grandmother ast me what I was thinkin while hangin like that. No way for me to say cause I can't clear remember any one thought comin behind another, thassa fact. Day by day I'm losin some more of what little I did remember. Night by night I be dreamin it over again, each time different. One night I dream Butler drop me and I was fallin straight down to get smattered on concrete. I woke up just in time, with such a jump till I fell outta bed.

When I was hangin from the roof, I do remember hearin a rock record playin on somebody's hi-fi, or else just playin in my head . . . group singin "Baby Don'tcha Leave Me." . . . Thassa blast! Like a movie, Jack! I could see the singin group every time I close my eyes, group poppin they fingers, doin fancy steps, dancin forward and back, makin circles. My mind had them guys wearin spensive lace shirts, gold pants, and green suede shoes; they was fine, real fine. When I open my eyes, I'm lookin up into Butler's face, veins in his face all swole out. I tried to think of my real father's face. Could remember a little bit of how he looked, but seem like real father's nose was narrower, keener than Butler's . . . also his eyes was some bigger . . . and the complexion brighter. Butler's face kept wipin out the real father. I believed that if I could see my real father's face, it could save my life.

Butler kept talkin, sayin mixed-up words, words, words . . . real father's face could not get through Butler's words, you dig? Butler keep sendin down them words, and they ain't nothin but sound goin like a-hunh-a-hunh-a-hunh like bees, insects hummin . . . and then it come to me that maybe I'm dyin and that's why faces and words meanin nothin. Then I feel my body beginnin to move up, up, up, sunshine hittin on Butler's face, makin a shiny light . . . light drawin tears to my eyes . . . like lookin straight into the sun. When light start dimmin down, Butler's face came through clear and plain . . . and I'm movin on up. Voice inside-a my head say, "Butler, you are my father." Thassa weird trip, Jack.

Yeah, I dig him. After all, the man save my life. People don't go round savin other people every day, you know, specially people they mad with. Sittin in that cold, wet snow felt good cause I was joyin bein alive. Ain't nothin wrong with alive ... if you gonna be somethin, be that!

My folks didden go to yellin at me like they can do sometime, no, they didden. They was glad bout me bein alive and well, everybody drowndin me with smiles, they really was. Middle of the night I woke up from the fallin-down dream and was hearin the voice again in my head: "Butler, you are my father." I got up shakin all over and wishin I had just a light skin pop to steady down my nerves, but I didden make one false move. I figured me a way to keep busy till the shakin pass. I wrote on a piece-a paper like how the teacher once gave me a hundred times to write—I WILL NOT ANSWER BACK— but, since this was me pushin myself, I wrote my own thing ... one hundred times: BUTLER IS MY FATHER ... BUTLER IS MY FATHER ... BUT-LER IS MY FATHER ... filled up both sides of my paper, two rows on each side, and had to sharpen the pencil two, three times. Was neat-lookin writin. Next thing I went out in the hall to where Butler's new coat is hangin on the rack ... and I fold that paper, put it in his pocket, then went on back to bed.

Come mornin. I'm feelin like a fool in the daylight, so I go to get the paper back ... but Butler wearin his coat, ready to go see a doctor bout his arm. Later, when he come back home, I say, "Butler, let me hang up your coat for you." That seem natural cause his arm in a sling now. He say, "Thank you, Benjie, my man." I go in both pockets while hangin the coat on the rack, but wassen no

paper, paper gone. I kept lookin at Butler's face to
see if he gonna laugh or go into a heart to heart or
what. The man got a straight face and *cool*. I'm
thinkin he crumple it up and threw it way cause
it mighta seem like a old candy wrapper or waste
paper. Whatever his faults, nobody can say the man
ain't cool.

* * *

Butler told Mama off bout takin me to Kenny's
funeral. Kenny's mama and mine both belong to the
union you have to belong to in order to sew in a
factory. Kenny's mother, by livin round the corner
from our house, used to come by when they both
had to be at union meetin, and like that.

Poor Kenny just turn fifteen and didden have
nothin else to do but get hold of a hot shot and die
of a overdose. Some tryin to say he was slipped a
hot shot on purpose cause he was meddlin with a
guy's sister, but that turn out to be a lie cause the
girl didden even know Kenny, except to see him
sometime walkin by. Fact is, I'm thinkin he had
been buyin and shootin weak doses that been cut
down to little or nothin, then he come cross a
strong deck, and it knocked on his heart. Anyhow,
whatever way it went, he's a dead cat now.

My mama made me go to Kenny's funeral with
her. I *had* to go. I'm on parole. They don't call it
that, but I gotta report to a social worker who's
workin with the youth court. If I don't show, they
will book me into a reform detention and charge
my family with negleck of a minor.

They be havin some tough laws and you better
ply yourself to givin up whatever you takin and
joinin with a program, or else you gonna be in a jail.

I gotta report to a caseworker what all I been doin since I last saw him.

A undertakin parlor is a weird place. Undertakin parlors have one kinda potted plant, palms like what you get on Palm Sunday in church, except undertakin palm is green and not yaller like church palm. People got to sign a book and put down they name and address fore they go up front to where the dead is laid out. I say to my mama, "I don't want to go look at him. I can see from back here."

"March," Mama say, "march up and look."

It seem impolite to stare at him when he's dead. No stuff, he helpless and he ain't able to look back at nobody who's lookin down at him. He look cold grayish brown, and hard as stone, and seem like his eyes and mouth glued together. He wearin a dumb square-lookin dark-blue suit, with a white carnation pinned to it. His hands folded cross his stomach, lookin pitiful, Jack. That casket is stone gray, and the inside part is white, shiny, satiny stuff like the linin of a lady's perfume box or like them Valentine chocolates. The whole scene look like it belong in a scary movie. Organ music playin, but you can't see no organ cause the man hidin behind a screen playin music that never come to a end; when you think it gonna end, it switch to another piece without stoppin.

Mama say, "Poor Kenny didn't get many flowers."

Look to me like enough, big fancy flowers standin up on wire legs. One was a wheel with a spoke missin, made outta red roses, a white ribbon bow with gold letters on it spell out TO OUR BELOVED KENNY. . . . There was another piece with the face of a clock set in the middle, time showin three o'clock. Mama say, "Uh, huh, that's the hour of his passin." How they know the hour of passin? They found him dead. The top half of the casket open, a lotta red carnations on the bottom part. Mama say, "Uh-huh, that is a half blanket-a flowers, really puttin him away right." All I'm thinkin is how Kenny was alive and laughin at Tiger's house. Mama would flip if she knew he gave me my first fix.

A lady sang a couple-a pieces and made people cry. Lady fat and short, her hair slicked back too tight, but she sing and hit them high notes without anybody having to wonder if she was gonna make it.

Kenny's mama hollered out, "Please God! Please help us!" I don't dig funerals. When people die, they oughta fade away so you can't see them no more, so they be gone without letting folks do all this to 'em. Tell you this, what I see sure don't make me look forward to bein dead.

There are numbers up on the wall, numbers of hymns people gotta sing. Preacher call out the number, you find it in the hymnbook, then rise and sing. Songs got no tune, people singin any kinda way and just goin la-la-hoo-hoo until they get down to Ahhhhhhhh-men, which is the end. Everybody cough like they in church, clearin they throat in a holy whisper. The minister waitin for coughin to be over, pattin his forehead and mouth with a white hankacha.

Mama copyin down the hymn number while people coughin. She say, "I have to put a quarter on this figure. Poor Kenny might bring me some luck." I wanta say, "He ain't brought hisself no luck, what make you think he gonna bring you some?" But I say nothin cause she the boss on everything since I'm on parole. But she shouldn't be thinkin bout winnin money at a time like this. If I was dead, it would hurt my feelins to think folks wanta play my hymn number.

I felt so glad when I step outta that undertaker parlor. Only disrespeck was three boys in the street, wearin purple jackets with green writin sayin "The Highest Eternal Avengers" ... they holdin signs, DEATH TO PUSHERS! KILL PUSHERS! I don't dig them uglyin up a funeral with signs. A couple-a times I delivered a deck for Walter, but I was not the real pusher myself. Glad I wasn't the one gave Kenny the overdose.

Insteada comin on home from in fronta the funeral, Mama gotta greet old folks, hug and kiss people, shake hands, and make me talk to em.

All say the same thing. "Mind now, you be a good boy and stay outta trouble." I say, "Yes, sir, yes, mam." I was glad Mama did not tell them bout me.

Jimmy-Lee there with his father, the old guy lookin dead as Kenny, clothes rumpled, eyes like they don't see nothin. Jimmy-Lee seem shamed of his dad, tryin to pull him to go home. People lookin at both of 'em. I feel sorry for Jimmy-Lee, I walk up and say, "Hey, my man." He look happy as a wagtail puppy.

"Where you been!" he say. "What you know!" When I was walkin off with Mama, he gave me a closed fist high sign and say, "Right on!" Jimmy-Lee got his ways, but he ain't the worst person in the world, you know.

Back home, Butler is mad at Mama for takin me to the funeral. He say, "You can't scare nobody into bein well. If you could, jails and hospitals all be empty."

Mama got mad when she find out Grandma told Butler bout the funeral and bout her givin me a bath in blue water from a fortune-teller. Mama hol-

lered at Grandma. "Why," she say, "why you have
to tell your guts to Butler? You talk bout him like
a dog and tell me not to tell him my business, but
soon as I turn my back, you shoot off your mouth.
You just a spoon stirrer in your old age, makin a I-
say-you-say between people. After all, you the one
asked me to go to the reader-adviser. Too bad she
didn't read and advise you to keep your mouth
shut."

Grandma stomp, drag her feet and start singin ...
"Precious Lord Take My Hand." ... She's goin to
her room. When she get to the door, she turn and
say, "I don't like how that fortune-teller talk bout
the Lord and dwellin on race and color. She was
sassy to Jesus! Even if Jesus is white, I'm made in
His image! Oh, how I love Him! If I gotta love
white, make mine Jesus!"

Butler, he too much. Butler laughin and say,
"Well, now, Mrs. Ransom Bell, who tole you Jesus
is white? Egypt, Jerusalem, all that parta the world
is Africa, fulla dark, nappy-headed folks. . . ."

Grandma say, "Shut up, sinner!" Then slam her
door shut.

Butler stop laughin and tole Mama, "Woman, I
don't wanta hear anymore about you goin to fortune-tellers or dealin in voo-doo. You're not gonna
be layin that out in fronta the social worker, so
don't be tryin no shortcuts to straightenin Benjie."

Mama punchin on the couch pillows like fluffin
them up, she's mad now. "Dammit," she say. "Kill
me! Why don't you and Benjie buy guns and shoot
me through the heart! His father could run, you
can run, he can run, even my mother can slam her
door; but I got to hold my ground and keep a roof
over our heads, clean house, put food on the table,
and also hit it on out here to work each and every

day. Dammit, get offa me! My name ain't 'Woman!'
I'm the one carin for Benjie and Mama, for better
or worse, and these days it's mostly worse. And my
name is still Johnson, not Craig!"

Butler say, "Hold on. I'm a man and you a
woman and he's a child ..."

Mama cut him off. "I be damn," she say. "We all
people before anything else. I'm somebody, too!
One these days women gonna learn to get up and
move, walk, and run out on everybody. How bout
that? Now I'm packin a bag and leavin all of you!
I'm movin out on family, the social worker, the police and schoolteachers! Yall figure the best way to
do everything!"

She flew in the bedroom and slam the french
door so hard till a piece-a glass fell out and smash
to the floor. She kickin things in the bedroom, ar-
guin so evil. I say to Butler, "You think she packin
her bag?"

Butler say, "No, but she wanta." He walk up and
down on the throw rug, then say, "Son, you drivin
the ladies crazy."

I say, "I'm sorry, Butler."

"Look here," he say. "Square your shoulders, admit you been a junkie, but now gonna stay clean
and report to daytime center for your followups. If
you don't do right, Butler gonna have to knock you
down, you hear?"

"I can do it," I say, "long as somebody believe in
me."

"Dammit, Benjie," he say, "you gotta do it even if
nobody believe in you, gotta be your own man, the
supervisor of your veins, the night watchman and
day shift foreman in charge-a your own affairs."

Butler pull me over to the window, and we

lookin down in the courtyard what's mixed up from people who throw garbage.

"Straighten up, Benjie," he say. "Do it even livin on the edge of ugly, cause we got nowhere else to go right now. Will you be sure and report to followup tomorrow?"

"Yeah," I say, "but you be there too."

"All right," he say, "I'll take off early, one more time."

"Right on, Butler," I say, "and I'll never ask you to promise me nothin else."

Butler throw back his head and laugh hearty, like he do, then say, "I promise you one thing more, Benjie, you not gonna be thirteen forever. You will someday be twenty-one, thirty-five and so on. Have patience. Soul doctor told me you not really hooked, just on the brink, you can draw back, you got it made, if you say so. How that strike you?"

"That strike me fine, Dad." Callin him dad slip out without thinkin. Sometime people say "dad" like usin slang, so I know that's what he thought I was meanin. But I stop being shame of what I say, so I say it again. "Fine, Dad. . . . Butler, you ain't the worst person in the world, you know."

He say, "Thank you." Butler lookin serious, and we standin at the window together, and he put his hand on my shoulder.

Mama is sweepin up busted glass from the floor. She say, "Who wants a piece-a pie and a glassa cold milk?" She smilin like nothin happen.

JIMMY-LEE'S FATHER

Street Corner Speaker

Hey, yall! Don't run by my stepladder so hasty. Where you hurryin to, the graveyard? I got somethin to tell you! Just saw a newborn baby girl who got here with a monkey on her back. Born hooked! Yall ready for that? Go in the hospital and ask if I'm lyin! Yeah, doctors had to drain out the blood from new little sister, had to fill her with new blood, blood from a stranger, to detox the brand-new infant child! Go ask the doctor to tell bout the many more gaspin their way into the world cryin and dyin for a fix! Got no home sweet home! Gotta send the baby to a *foster* home cause mom and dad on the nod . . . and done messed up the seed!

Yall must don't mind! Yall think skag is prosperity. Heartbreak, five bucks a bag! Whitey chargin us money to off ourselves, niggas out here hustlin for him! Look at brothers and sisters bent low, knees knocked together to keep from fallin on their ass, hangin over with hands clenched into helpless fists. DIG HOW TO KILL A NIGGA WITHOUT FIRING A GUN! Teach him to kill hisself! Teach him to latch a monkey on baby's back fore baby draws breath. Brothers, your *honor* got to be more than somethin you call a judge! Look at the gray-haired sisters fraid to walk home, scared the strong young men gonna jump em, knock em in the head, snatch pocketbooks, and cut throats. Look up at the sky; whitey has walked out on space while our noses pointin down, on the nod! They lookin for a new neighborhood, dig? They have so demoralized the world, till it ain't fit to live in ... poisoned the air, the streams, rivers and oceans, the earth and all that's in it, and the mind and body of man! Bible say the meek shall inherit the earth! We meek ain't gonna be gettin very much if the earth keep on keepin on like it is!

The children now risin up, but not to call you blessed! Hear me! Hear me! Them that's tryin to kick the habit, now crawlin to the one who put it on em ... sayin. "Please, Massa, hold my hand and help me shake off my monkey." Look at em walking to the detox center where they can get a little taste-a somethin else to ease off skag. Go to hell, man! You can't get angry, cause you *numb*, can't feel a-tall. Walk on, man, damn your coward soul! I gave yall my life ... now I'm standin before you, a money less, broke down son of Nat Turner ... I got nothin left but breath in my body ... here it go ... take all of me ... all I got left to offer the race ... breath, breath ... Freeeeeeedom now! Freeeeeeeeeeeeeeedom now!

BUTLER CRAIG

Nothin really works until the boy *wants* to kick and report to the center on his own free will. Well, Benjie sure wants to, so we ahead of the game so far. Here I am waitin out in the street for the second damn time, but, after all, a promise can't always be kept the first time around.

Had to get me another few days off from work. That's no big thing because the time can come offa my vacation. After all, I did get picked, by Benjie, to be his father one hundred times. A chosen man so to speak. Well, some might say that me and circumstances ain't quite good enough for the job. But I know better. I can do what social worker, head shrink and blood kin can't—give a boy back to himself, so he can turn man. You better believe it.

We've had us a few days happier than any ever before, days that came out right and Sweets now startin her divorce action on groundsa desertion. Last night, after supper, me and Benjie went to playin records, laughin, and havin us a natural ball. Even Mrs. Ransom Bell got caught up when Benjie say, "Dance, Grandma! When you ever gonna do your dance?" Wow! Mrs. Ransom Bell snatches her dress right up to the knee and counts off, "A-one and a-two and a-three." Then damn if she didn't go into a quiverin shake that's not to be believed, shook and shivered bout half a minute, went into a time step, then did a off-to-Buffalo that took her right to her room. We standin there speechless till we start to applaudin, then she close her door and went to singin "Rock of Ages" in top voice. Mrs. Ransom Bell is too much, she really is, cracks me up.

It's gettin cold standin here waitin for Benjie. First I was in the entranceway, but it came to me that Benjie wouldn't be able to see me if he was comin from the corner; if he can't see, he might go away and not try again later. Out here on the steps he can see me from both ends of the street. No way he can mistake me for somebody else, cause my arm is still in the sling ... and stiff as a board. Doctor say a sprain can be worse than a break. All that roof action is hard on the joints.

I better stand out near the curb edge so he can be sure it's me. Damn. I could haul off and hit some-a these head shrinks and social workers, hit them full on, fist against front teeth. We've been followin their say-so and advice the way the apostles followed Jesus. Day before yesterday, a shrink told Sweets it was bad how we never let Benjie make any decisions or have responsibility, so I gave him money to go in a store alone to buy a suit. Dig, he came home yesterday *wearin* the new outfit, with his old clothes wrapped in a box. I cracked up! sweets cussed him, but I laughed till tears rolled down my cheeks. He had bought a *orange* suit with brown velvet lapels. Look like he was dressed in rotten orange peelins. Blew fifty-seven fifty on that cheap-Charlie suit. The cloth wrinklin and bucklin at the knee ... and he ain't had it on but half hour. Truth is, reason I didn't get mad like Sweets ... I was glad he didn't buy skag with the money. I was

proud to see him do what he promised to do, even if
it was done wrong.

I wish I could see that orange suit turnin the corner right now. Some-a these head shrinks got
brass-ass, cold nerve, they don't know how close to
a word-whippin they get when talkin rehab with
me. I been learnin to button my lip and take stuff
offa them that I wouldn't even take from Mrs. Ransom Bell. Today the adviser told me Benjie needs
"some male hero figure he can identify with," then
goes to showin me a lista books bout Black History
also tellin bout "colored" movie stars and great
sports figures and how I must take Benjie to movies
and ball games so he can see more heroes.

I gave the adviser some advice. I say, "Some
these big-time, celebrity-high-lifers can't take care-
a themselves, they in as much trouble as you and
Benjie. Yall gotta learn to identify with *me*, who
gotta get up to face the world every damn mornin
with a clear head and a heavy heart. Benjie once
told me a hero ain't nothin but a sandwich—and
you say a hero is a celebrity! Litsen to *my* creden-
tials; then maybe yall can pin me on a hero button.
I'm supportin three adults, one chile, and the
United States government on my salary ... and
can't claim any of em for tax exemptions. So, explain me no heroes. Yeah, and some-a our neighborhood success stories are livin offa Benjie's veins,
while they ridin round in limousines and grand-
standin to win everybody's admiration!

A half-ass *Negro* guard then takes my arm and
walks me toward the door, sayin, "Hush now,
brother."

I had somethin for him too. I say, "Don't ease me
out the door with that brother talk. Get your hand
off me, man."

This skag trouble and the rehab has open up a whole new look at life for me.

Yeah, I'm out here standin in fronta the addict center. This is me! Musician fella I know passed by and say, "Butler, man, what you doin?"

I say, "Standin, waitin for my son, that's what."

Fella knew by my tone that he's to leave the subject *alone* and not ask anything else. So that's what he did. Yeah, I'm standin and waitin. It don't pay to get restless and leave cause a child is little bit late. Kids really don't have a good sense-a time. Benjie likes to look in store windows. Lotsa times I say, "Benjie, come on, stop lookin in windows or we'll be late." Bet that's what he's doin now ... lookin in windows. I would take a walk up to the corner and see if he's lingerin on the avenue, but that'd be the time he'd come from the other way and think I didn't show up. But won't hurt to go to the other side-a the street so it'll give me a better view of the corners on this side, also be no way for me to miss him. I know that he'll be here, but I sure wish he'd come on.

The wind is blowing colder now, but if I go in— he might get this far, then lose courage. Come on, Benjie, I believe in you ... Benjie, don't hold back, come on, I'm waitin for you ... hurry up, I'm waitin, boy ... I'm waitin right here ... It's nation time ... I'm waitin for you. ...

ABOUT THE AUTHOR

Alice Childress is a writer, actress, and director. She brings her theatrical experience to the novel in characterization and dialogue.

Her play *Wedding Band* was presented during the 1972-73 season by Joseph Papp's Public Theatre, *Trouble in Mind* received the Obie Award for the best off-Broadway production of 1955-56, and a third play, *Wine in the Wilderness,* was presented on NET. Many of her plays have been anthologized, and she is the author of a number of stories and articles which have appeared in *Freedomways, Essence,* and *The Black World.* She is the editor of *The Black Scene,* a collection of fifteen scenes from works by Black playwrights.

Miss Childress was born in Charleston, South Carolina, and grew up and attended school in Harlem. She was a member of the American Negro Theatre for ten years. From 1966 to 1968, she received a Harvard appointment to the Radcliffe Institute. She is a community-elected board member of the Francis Delafield City Hospital and a member of the Harlem Writers Guild and the New Dramatists. She has traveled widely in the USSR and Europe and recently visited mainland China.